Eerey Tocsin
and the Invisible Tower

The Tocsin Codex: Book III

Coding by Kevin Noel Olson
Hieroglyphs by Debi Hammack

Eerey Tocsin and the Invisible Tower
The Tocsin Codex: Book III
by Kevin Noel Olson

A Cornerstone Book
Published by Cornerstone Book Publishers
Story Copyright © 2010 by Kevin Noel Olson
Illustrations Copyright © 2010 by Debi Hammack

Cornerstone Book Publishers
New Orleans, LA

First Cornerstone Edition - 2010

www.cornerstonepublishers.com

ISBN: 1613422245
ISBN-13: 978-1-61342-224-3

MADE IN THE USA

Dedication

I dedicate this too my wife, my family, and my friends. I love you beyond what can be adequately expressed, and beyond what time may encase.

-K.N.O.

In the timing of the sand, I seem to feel
a cosmic time: all the long history
That memory keeps sealed up in its mirrors
Or that has been dissolved by magic Lethe.

- Jorges Luis Borges

Introduction

It is with great apprehension that I write this introduction to the third book detailing Eerey's adventures. To date, I have not received word from anyone from or connected to Eridona 'Eerey' Tocsin or her family. It is my sincere hope that they are all safely residing in some far-off land, enjoying inclement weather.

I received a copy of Eerey's diary by postal delivery. The plain, brown envelope in which it came contained no return address. I have attempted to verify the details of the story without significant success. Nevertheless, the publisher is eagerly awaiting this volume. No objective proof or further evidence is currently available to me. The story seems to be missing important details, which to me, adds to its authenticity. I cannot afford to wait any longer. I will present it is as I am aware of it today.

There are small, circumstantial evidences of time travel and the planet Monstrator to corroborate what is said in the diary. The Dorchester Pot, for example, seems to suggest that someone carried a modern trinket into the past and planted it there to be later discovered. Perhaps Eerey herself placed it? I do not know. I will add that I was able to track down the antique store that might have sold the sunglasses Eerey said she lost in the first book. The owner of the store recalled selling sunglasses to someone fitting the description of Eerey's mother. It was inferred to me as possible that they were discovered with the Dorchester Pot, but this remains unsubstantiated.

More of Eerey's diary may come to light in the future and explain this strange object. Today, the story is mostly conjecture. All I can say for certain is what I have been able to confirm about

Eerey's diaries have all proven to be fact. Also, I have never been dissuaded to doubt her integrity. Please enjoy this story as presented, and be assured I will report any further information that comes to light regarding the adventures.

Sincerely,
Kevin Noel Olson
August the 17th, 2010

Eerey Tocsin
and the Invisible Tower

The Tocsin Codex: Book III

CHAPTER 1

ROSANANTE'S MUMMY

Eerey smiled as she opened the hatch leading outside the former bomber. Former meaning a plane no longer used to deliver bombs. It retired from that duty in the 1940s. Now, it delivered cargo. Now, it flew high over the ocean. Engines droned in steady rhythm as the wind whipped over the wings.

The young girl named Eridona Tocsin looked through her shaded goggles darkly. She wore the goggles to protect her eyes from the sunlight and the rushing air. The wind whipped her long red hair as she looked at the water far below and shuddered. She pulled the belt around her waist to test the line hooked securely to it. She allowed a wry grin to cross her lips.

A black spider the size of a bowling-ball crawled over the plane's wing toward the young girl. Eerey reached a hand toward the spider.

"Come here, Eightball. That's a good boy!"

The spider wrapped its legs around her extended arm. She pulled the attached arachnid and her arm into the plane. The door slammed shut against the rushing air. It slammed shut. She set the spider on the floor. Eightball rolled over onto his back, extending eight legs into the air. The arachnid displayed the white figure-eight marking on its belly.

Eerey smiled. "You want me to scratch your belly, don't you?" Without waiting for a reply she reached out and began petting the symbol. She looked at the sleeve of her thick, striped mechanic's jacket. It was torn to shreds where Eightball held onto her arm. "You really tore up the jacket," she tsked. "Looks like you tried to bite me, too! I don't hope to find out if you're poisonous or not that way, you know!"

She smiled at Eightball. The spider let out a purr (or growl) at the petting of his belly. She stopped petting the spider and walked toward the pilot's cabin. Her mother flew the airplane as Eerey walked in.

"Mother," Eerey said, "why are you still wearing that mask?"

Mrs. Tocsin's dark hair flowed over her pilot's jacket. "We might run into another pocket of gas."

Eerey took the dark goggles off and put her sunglasses on. "If we do, shouldn't we all be wearing masks?"

Her father, in the co-pilot's chair, shook his head. "No," he said, his voice muffled by the gas mask. "It's not necessary at any rate. The methane gas probably wouldn't kill you, but if the pilots go unconscious the entire plane might crash."

Eerey rolled her eyes. "As long as it *probably* won't kill us. How much farther is it to Lydia?"

Eerey's mother tapped the instrument panel. "According to these readings, the compass and odometer are both entirely askew. That and the fact we have no idea what direction we are headed, I'd have to say there is no way of knowing for certain."

Looking out his window, Mister Tocsin nodded. "That's right. We don't know."

Eerey crossed her arms. "We don't know a lot of things. We don't know what happened to Guy Guess, the invisible boy. We don't know why Mister Cryptic is mummified in a huge metal sarcophagus shaped like a horse. Not knowing where we are adds another mystery to figure out."

Mrs. Cryptic nodded. "That's why we are going to Lydia, so we can figure out all those things." She sighed. "Hopefully we find it soon. We are nearly out of fuel."

Eerey rolled her eyes. "We can't figure out how to get to Lydia by getting there first. We've got to figure that out before we can get to Lydia, not after."

Mister Tocsin nodded. "That's true, but once we get there we'll know *how* to get there."

The sound of horse shoes clattered in long, slow strides from the rear of the plane. "Sounds like Loofah's headed to the pilot's compartment."

True to Eerey's prophesy, Loofah the orangutaur stepped into the compartment. His orangutan torso and head rested upon body and legs of a Shetland pony. He placed his gangly orangutan arms on his horse hips and sighed deeply.

"Hey!" Eerey complained. "You're making it a bit crowded in here! Did you want something?"

The orangutaur repeated his sigh. "Not really. I just got tired of standing around in the back. Edict drones on and on about nothing interesting. He can be such a boor."

"It's boorish to crowd the pilots," Eerey noted.

Loofah nodded as he thoughtlessly shifted and pressed the girl into her mother. "That's what I mean. It's exactly the kind of thing

Edict would do."

Eerey used both hands to push the intruding orangutaur. "I'm talking about you, you big lug! Are you dense?"

Loofah felt his arm. "Yes," he nodded. "I suppose I am dense. I'm not light as a feather." He shrugged. "I can't fly, for example. I sink like a rock in water unless I swim."

Eerey gritted her teeth. "Keep it up, and we'll see if you can swim through the air!"

Through the gas mask, Mrs. Tocsin suggested, "Perhaps both of you should leave. We have a plane to pilot, you know. You are causing a distraction."

Loofah sighed. "Well, I could go back and watch Mister Cryptic's metal sarcophagus. It's glowing with an eerie green light. Pretty cool, really."

"What!?" Eerey asked as she tried to push her way past the orangutaur. "Why didn't you say? I have to see this!"

Loofah backed out of the compartment. "I didn't know you needed to see," he explained. "Edict said to tell you, but I thought he was being a boor."

Eerey pushed Loofah aside. "Let's go see!"

Loofah stepped outside the pilot's compartment. "No need to rush," he said. "It's probably still glowing. It's been doing it for fifteen minutes."

Eerey shook her head as she headed for the cargo area. "It took you and Edict that long to think to tell me? It could be important!"

Loofah nodded. "That's why we didn't want to miss it. When I got bored watching it glow I came up here."

Eerey rushed toward the cargo area. She turned the handle to the door and rushed in. Edict stood next to the large metal horse. "Don't stand there growing more hair!" Eerey said to her cousin, referring to the fact Edict was covered in blonde hair from toe to top.

"Tell me what happened."

"Okay," Edict said. "The horse started glowing green."

"Is that all?"

Edict scratched his head. "Did you want more?"

Eerey looked at the glowing metal horse. "Yes. A little consideration would be nice. You know I would want to see this."

Edict asked, "Do you think the glow is radiation? It could be dangerous."

Eerey tilted her head. "It might be deadly."

Loofah walked in. "Is anything exciting happening?"

Eerey nodded. "Rosanante is glowing green."

"Rosanante?" Edict repeated.

"Rosanante was Don Quixote's old horse," Eerey explained.

Loofah scratched his chin. "Don Quixote?"

Eerey sighed. "Forget it. The big metal horse is glowing, and I've dubbed her Rosanante."

"We'll get radiation sickness is what I think," Loofah said.

"Do you feel ill?" Eerey asked.

"No," Loofah admitted, "but I saw it happen to this guy on television once."

Eerey rolled her eyes. "That's scientific."

"Not really," Edict said.

"I was being sarcastic."

"Sarcastic?" Loofah repeated. "Is that like a sarcophagus?"

Eerey shrugged. "No. It could lead to that though."

The plane jostled violently, throwing Edict against the glowing sarcophagus. Loofah remained standing as he slid across the floor, horseshoes sparking. Eerey held onto the door to keep from falling.

"What was that?" Eerey asked everything calmed down.

"I dunno." Loofah moved over to a window while Eerey went to check on Edict.

Eerey pulled at his legs to get him out of the glow. "Are you alright Edict?"

Her hair-covered cousin smiled broadly and dusted off his flight jacket. "Yeah, I'm okay."

"But…you're glowing!" Eerey said.

Edict looked at his hairy hands. "I am glowing green like the sarcophagus!" The boy smiled broadly. "Neat!"

"Not 'neat', cousin," Eerey said. "It could be deadly!"

Edict shrugged. "So could that stupid spider you carry around."

"He's not stupid!" Eerey said.

Edict repeated his shrug. "You have a big spider. I'm glowing green. I like it, and you like your spider. People gotta like different things."

"You shouldn't be glowing green from a gold sarcophagus," Loofah said. "It makes no sense!"

Edict nodded. "Sure it does. Golden wheat starts out green when it's young, doesn't it?"

Eerey pushed her sunglasses up. "Whatever. We should have you checked out."

Loofah continued staring out the window. "I don't think we have that much time."

Eerey moved to an adjacent, round window. "What do you mean…oh…"

A metal horse flew next to the airplane. It looked identical to Mister Cryptic's sarcophagus except the copper color of its metal and red glow. "It's another sarcophagus!" Edict said.

Eerey shook her head. "It's not a sarcophagus-it's some kind of aircraft. Or a spaceship. Usually, sarcophagi don't usually fly as fast a B-17."

Loofah looked at the metal horse holding Mister Cryptic. "Maybe that's a spaceship too!"

"Congratulations," Eerey said, still watching the copper craft. "Collect your door prize on the way out."

Loofah shook his head. "I'm not leaving yet. Orangutaur's fly best inside an airplane. I've got four legs and two arms. I don't have wings."

"Neither does that flying metal sarcophagus," Edict nodded out the window. "How is it flying, anyway? I don't see any engines."

Eerey shrugged. "It's flying, that's all. It's hard to say how. It doesn't look like it could. They say a bee doesn't look like it can fly either."

Loofah peered out the window. "I think it's using some type of anti-gravity."

"Whatever that means," Edict said.

"That means," Eerey sighed, "it defies gravity. The airplane does that."

Loofah nodded. "Sure. I read about anti-gravity in an alien comic. I mean a comic about aliens. But we know why the airplane flies-air resistance."

"We still don't know how the sarcophagus flies," Eerey said.

"Shush!" Edict said, pressing his hairy, glowing face into the round window, "the sarcophagus is shooting a red ray at us!"

CHAPTER II

THE SARCOPHAGUS COUGHS

They all watched intently as the red laser or beam of light struck the airplane. The outside of the airplane glowed with the same bright-red light as a translucent red sphere of light enveloped it. They backed away from the windows.

"Ouch!" Edict said, rubbing his eyes with his hairy fingers. "That hurts my eyes!"

Tears trickled out from under Eerey's goggles. "Mine too."

As their eyes adjusted to the light, they returned to the window. Although the plane still flew forward, the propellers ceased spinning.

"The propellers aren't spinning!" Edict stated the obvious. "That's bad!" He again stated the obvious. "We can't defy gravity without them!"

"That's obvious!" Eerey said. "Don't be obtuse!"

Edict's face fell. "Obtuse? I'm not a square!"

"Obtuse means slow." Eerey said.

After a moment, Edict said, "I'm not slow!"

Eerey nodded. "So, don't be. The propellers aren't spinning. That means we are not flying under our own power and we could crash."

Loofah sighed. "That's typical. It's not even lunchtime."

"What's that got to do with it?" Eerey asked.

"If it was after lunch," Loofah said, "At least I'd die with a full stomach!"

Eerey shook her head. "I don't think we're going to crash. The copper sarcophagus seems to be towing us."

"Huh," Edict said. "I think you're right, cuz."

"Why do you think that, Edict?" Loofah asked.

"Maybe," Eerey suggested, "because we're still flying and not headed down." The three looked down at the ocean.

"The waves are going backward!" Loofah exclaimed.

"How do you know?" Edict asked.

"Look how they end evenly the way a wave starts. They seem to start with a full-formed, foamy wave!"

Eerey agreed. "It does look like that."

Edict pointed at the sky. "Look! The sun's stopped!"

Eerey nearly cracked her head and the glass. "That's not possible! You can't tell if the sun's stopped!" Her eyes began to water from staring at it.

Edict began glowing brighter. "The sun's rays aren't moving! It's like a photo!"

Loofah coughed. "It's moving again, away from us! It's moving fast too!"

Eerey nodded. "We were moving with it. Now, it's moving away, and quickly!"

They all stood aghast as they watched the orb move away from the ship. "What can it mean?" Edict asked.

Eerey shrugged. "It doesn't make sense, unless we're moving through time."

"Or the sun is," Loofah suggested.

"That's not likely," Eerey said. "It's easier to move a bomber through time than an entire solar system."

Edict shook his head. "We don't need to know what's happening. We need to know what we can do about it."

"I don't think we can do anything about it," Loofah said.

"I don't know," Eerey said, "if we should do anything about it. Let's see what happens."

A deep, hollow cough came from the mouth of Mr. Cryptic's metallic horse. It then began to speak. "You do need to know what is transpiring. Or what is untranspiring, as the case may be."

They turned to the green-glowing sarcophagus in surprise. Eerey spoke first. "What did you say? Who are you, anyway?"

"I'll answer your second question first. I am Mister Cryptic, of course. Now your first question I'll answer second. Events are untranspiring. Many events happen, yet the ship is moving through the events that could have occurred, yet did not. The possibility exists, and we travel through one of the infinite, untranspired realities."

Loofah scratched his front hoof against the metal floor. "How can we move through events that did not exist?"

"Stop that, Loofah!" Edict said.

"Scratching my hoof?"

"No. Stop asking obtuse questions." Edict turned to Eerey and smiled.

The horse answered Loofah's question. "Think of a pair of unplugged lamps next to an outlet. One has a bulb that is burned out and is red. The other light has a green bulb that works. Edict, say you are in another room and Loofah chooses to plug one in. Being in the other room, you cannot see which one he chose to plug in. To you, the light is simultaneously burned out and red and on and green. Both possibilities exist until you know which one is or isn't."

"Like Schrodinger's cat," Eerey said.

"An appropriate analogy," the metal horse replied, "though a bit morbid compared to my example."

"You are a mummy in a sarcophagus," Eerey reminded. "Perhaps not the best judge of what's morbid."

"Who's Schrodinger," Edict asked, "and what about his cat?"

"The story is not important," Eerey said. "Basically, it's an experiment with a cat in a box and a bottle of poison gas. If the bottle falls over and breaks, it releases the gas and the cat is dead. If it does not, the cat is alive. From a scientific standpoint, the cat's both dead and alive until you look in the box."

"A Frankencat?" Loofah said. "That is morbid!"

Eerey shrugged. "I doubt Schrodinger tested it."

"What if you had the box x-rayed?" Loofah asked.

Eerey sighed. "That's looking inside the box now, isn't it?"

"So, the cat is kind of like the lamp?" Edict said. "Yeah, I think the metal horse is right. It's pretty morbid."

Eerey sighed. "Okay, so it's morbid. The metal horse is right."

"I am Mister Cryptic," the horse corrected. "I am inside the metal horse, but I am speaking. And I am right. That is why Loofah saw the waves untranspiring."

"So," Loofah began, "things are untranspiring?"

The sarcophagus didn't shake its horse-head as Mister Cryptic spoke. "No. We are travelling in impossible energy. That's energy that does not exist because it remains uncreated."

"Sound kinda negative," Edict said.

"It is not negative," Mister Cryptic replied. "It is simply

untranspiring. Something transpiring is not necessarily positive, as something untranspiring is not necessarily negative."

Loofah nodded. "You mean that, if something bad doesn't happen, that's good. Right?"

"Basically," the metal horse replied. "It's pretty mundane, really."

"Perhaps," Eerey said, "but travelling through time is not mundane. It's pretty weird, actually."

"I don't agree," Mr. Cryptic disagreed. "People travel through time constantly. You cannot help it even if you stood still. Granted, travelling backward through time is weird. It is especially if you have not done so before."

"You're pretty smart for a horse statue," Loofah said.

"I am not a statue," Mr. Cryptic protested. "I am Mister Cryptic."

Loofah looked through a round port in the side of the sarcophagus. "Your lips aren't moving when you talk."

"I am speaking," the horse-head said, "with telepathy. I think so you can hear my thoughts, and you think you do."

Loofah shook his head. "I think that's what you want us to think." Loofah stood up and looked at Eerey. "I don't think it is Mister Cryptic talking or the metal horse."

Eerey looked out the window at the flying metal horse. "Do you think it's them?"

Edict shrugged. "If anyone can talk to us and hypnotize us with their minds, I'll bet distance doesn't matter."

Eerey nodded. "I suppose."

"It is me!" the horse head replied. "I am Mister Cryptic!"

Eerey walked out of the room and returned with a screw-lid glass jar filled with water. Inside rested an oyster with duct tape over its shell. "I think it could be Pen."

The oyster vibrated a little. "No!" the horse head said. "Pay no attention to the oyster in the Mason jar! I am Mister Cryptic!"

Eerey unscrewed the lid on the jar. "You claimed you were Mister Cryptic when we first met you," Eerey reminded as she pulled the oyster out of the jar.

"I am Mister Cryptic!" the metal horse-head protested. The oyster dripped water on the floor as it struggled to open its taped shell.

Eerey began to peel away the duct tape. "Stop talking through the horse, Pen. I know it's you. Things are confusing enough already."

Loofah held his hand out in dramatic, traffic-control fashion. "Don't take his tape off Eerey!"

The tape peeled away as Eerey said, "Why? What will he do? Bite me? Oysters don't have teeth!"

The oyster sunk its teeth into Eerey's wrist. "Ow!" The oyster fell to the floor and slid under the sarcophagus.

Edict shook his head. "Oysters don't have teeth. You forgot doppelganger's have sharp teeth."

Loofah retrieved a roll of gauze and a bottle of iodine from the first aid cabinet attached to the wall. "Here," he said. He began to pour iodine on the wound and wrap it. "That could get infected."

"Hey!" the metal horse protested. "I don't carry diseases!"

"Guess that answers the question as to who is making the horse talk," Eerey said as she took over the job of wrapping of her wounded wrist. "Someone should grab the oyster."

Laughter rang in Eerey's ears. She looked up to see who laughed, seeing her father standing there in his gas mask and flight suit. "No oyster any longer," the fake Mr. Tocsin said.

"Dad!" Eerey rubbed her bandaged wrist.

"No," Pen replied. "I am not an oyster, nor your father."

Edict stepped next to Eerey. "How did you get dad's DNA?" he asked.

Pen's muffled voice laughed beneath the gas mask. "Don't you know? Eerey has her father's DNA already!"

Eerey nodded. "I never thought of that before. I suppose it's possible you can turn into our parents with our DNA."

Pen shook his head. "It's not only possible. I just did it! Not just your parents. I can go as far back into your ancestry as I want."

"When did you figure that out?" Loofah asked.

"Just now," Pen admitted. "Still, it is a pretty neat trick. Do you not think so?"

Edict grinned at Loofah. "He doesn't think if he doesn't have to."

Loofah smiled. "I have to," he replied, "anytime you're around. Someone has to keep you from hurting yourself."

"Knock it off you two," Eerey said. "We've got other things to deal with," She sighed, "too many confusing things at once."

"Yeah," Loofah agreed. "I'm getting a headache."

"I'll go get dad," Edict said as he walked out of the room.

"It won't do any good," Pen said, crossing his arms. He turned to Loofah and Eerey. "He'll be back."

They stood patiently as Edict returned in a few seconds. "They aren't moving!" he reported.

"What!?" Eerey walked to the front compartment and looked in. The red sphere separated the pilot compartment from the rest of the ship, yet she could see her parents stiff as wax figures. She walked back to the cargo area. "They're stock still."

"Remember," Edict said, "you heard it from me first."

"Not exactly," Pen said. "I believe it would not be incorrect to say, I told you so."

CHAPTER III

MOUNTAIN CRASH

Edict nodded. "You may have told us that our parents weren't moving, Pen. You didn't tell us something even more important."

Pen's rolled his eys under the gas mask. "What's that?"

"We're headed for a mountain," Edict replied. "We'll crash into it!"

A pearl rolled out from under Pen's gas mask. "We can't do that!"

The three rushed after Edict as he led them to the pilot's compartment. He halted just in front of the wall of bright, reddish light and blocked the others. "Stop! We can't go through the sphere's wall!"

"Why not?" asked Loofah.

"Because we'll become frozen like them!" Eerey replied.

"How do we know if we haven't tried it?" Loofah replied.

"Do you want to try it?" Edict asked.

Loofah shook his head. "After you, Edict. After you."

"Someone needs to try something!" Eerey said.

Loofah opened a storage closet and began rifling through its contents. "Is there time to parachute out of the plane?"

"Probably not," Eerey said.

Pen laughed. "It is fun watching you all killing yourselves with excitement, but I have to tell you there's nothing to worry about. We won't crash."

Eerey turned toward the gas-masked Pen. "How do you know?"

Pen shrugged. "Trust me."

Loofah rolled his eyes as he continued seeking parachutes. "That's never worked for us before."

Pen repeated his shrug. "Fine. Don't trust me, then."

"We can't trust you on that, either," Eerey said. "You could be giving us bad advice. Either we trust you, or we don't trust you. Somehow, I think we'll regret both."

Edict sighed. "I think we're out of time to regret either."

To confirm his estimation, the mountain loomed in front of the airplane. Everyone, including Pen, held their arms in front of their eyes. Eerey took note of this.

"I thought you said we wouldn't crash, Pen!" she said.

"There's still a chance I'm right!" Pen shouted back. The pearl he'd spit earlier rolled to his black dress shoe and bounced off with a clattering sound. He shrugged. "There's a chance I'm wrong too!"

Loofah peeked out with his left eye before slamming it shut again. "Not much time now for any more chances!"

The nose of the plane met the surface of the mountain. A crackling sound of thunder filled the airplane. Eerey opened her eyes to see the red wall of energy had disappeared. Her parents were moving as normal, and the sky turned pitch black.

CHAPTER IV

BLIND LANDING

Pen nodded. "I told you we would not crash. The mountain was an illusion. At least I thought so."

Eerey's mother turned on the cabin lights. "What happened!? The sky's gone dark!"

Eerey's father turned on the plane's outside lights. "I don't know," he replied, "but we need to land soon. We're out of fuel!"

Eerey rushed forward. "Turn off the outside lights!" she told Mister Tocsin.

Mister Tocsin turned his gas-masked face to his daughter. "What are you talking about Eerey!?"

"Trust me, dad." Eerey turned to Mrs. Tocsin as she looked at

Eerey. "I can see in the dark! Let me guide you! I saw a place to land, but I can't see it with the lights on!"

Mrs. Tocsin nodded her gas-masked face her husband. "Trust her, Victor."

Victor shrugged as he turned off the lights. "Okay Verna. It's all up to you now Eerey."

Eerey went to the windshield and peered out. "Okay dad. Slow down as if you're coming in for a landing and steer slightly to the right. There's an invisible skyscraper there."

"Invisible!?" Mr. Tocsin said. "How can you see it?"

Eerey gritted her teeth. "Just do it dad."

Victor was already doing so. "Okay?"

Eerey's took off the dark goggles and continued to peer. Her face scrunched in concentration. "Just a little bit more to the right. Good! That's it! Now, descend as if you're coming in for a landing. That's it!"

Mr. Tocsin steadied the plane. "How much of a runway do I have? We need a lot!"

Eerey shrugged. "How much? It looks like a long rooftop!"

Mr. Tocsin shrugged. "We need at least a couple of football fields."

Eerey gulped. "What if I told you you're not getting half that?"

"I'd tell you we're probably done for," Eerey's dad replied. "Are you saying that's all we've got?"

Eerey looked about at the rugged, rocky terrain. She turned to walk out of the compartment. "I'm saying we will get enough! Land the plane as if we do."

"Where are you going, Eerey!?" Verna demanded. "We need you to guide us so we can land!"

"I'm going to make the runway long enough!" Eerey said. "You're going to need it longer so you can land!"

Victor turned to Verna. "Does that mean it's not long enough?"

Verna shrugged. "It means it has to be long enough. Either it is or it isn't."

Pen, Loofah, and Edict followed Eerey as she headed for the cargo area. "We've got to wake up Mister Cryptic!"

"What good will that do?" Loofah asked.

"We won't know until we do it!" Edict replied.

"We might not even know after that," Pen replied.

Eerey nodded in agreement. "No, we might not know. We've got to try. If the red sarcophagus could drag us here, maybe Mister Cryptic's might be able to slow us down!"

"Where are we?" Loofah asked.

"If we crash," Edict reminded, "it won't matter."

"I'd still like to know," the orangutaur grumbled.

Eerey walked over to the sarcophagus and started banging on the sides with her palms. The metal echoed loudly as she shouted, "Wake up, Mister Cryptic! We need you!"

The sarcophagus began to glow again.

CHAPTER V

AN UNTRANSIRED PLANE CRASH

A voice came from the glowing sarcophagus. "Is that you Eerey?" it asked. The plane's engines sputtered as they ran out of fuel.

Eerey nodded and backed away from the glowing sarcophagus. "Yes, it's me. Is it really you Mister Cryptic?" She glanced at Pen, still looking like Eerey's father in a gas mask.

The voice yawned. "Yes, it is. What can I do for you?"

"You can keep us from crashing," Eerey suggested. "I'd appreciate not dying."

The voice from the sarcophagus fell silent while precious seconds ticked away. "Ah, yes," Mr. Cryptic said at last. "I see the problem.

Why can't you do it yourself, Eerey?"

"I don't see how I can," Eerey replied.

"We can't!" Loofah said. "That's obvious!"

"It may be obvious Loofah," Mr. Cryptic said. "That does not mean it is impossible. Very, very little is impossible given the right circumstances." The voice from the metal horse sighed.

"We don't have time for a philosophical discussion!" Eerey objected. "There's not enough time to convince my dad it's not dark, because the mountain isn't real so he can see! You've got to stop us from crashing!"

Mr. Cryptic sighed again. "I have already done that."

Eerey rushed to look out the window with the others.

"How can you do that?" Edict asked. "It sounds impossible!"

"If you look at them closely, most things sound impossible," Mr. Cryptic explained. "If you look at the reality, I have made what sounds impossible become fact."

Loofah furrowed his brow. "You made the plane land?"

No one could see Mr. Cryptic shake his head in the sarcophagus, so they did not know if he shook his head or not. "No," Mr. Cryptic replied. "I just set the plane down on the roof when it was not moving."

Loofah sighed. "I've tried to understand you, Mister Cryptic. It makes my head hurt, so I gave up. I just want off this plane."

"By all means," Mr. Cryptic said. "You should leave. My energy is depleting. I can't hold the plane stationary in time forever, you know."

"What about our parents?" Edict asked.

"I will take the plane and your parents to safety." Mr. Cryptic said. "It's easiest to take it back to where it came from than to keep it here. Not to mention I need to spend the energy to remove the other time-bubble."

Loofah shook his head and furrowed his brow. "This still doesn't make any sense!"

Eerey sighed and waved her arm. "Let's get out of here."

Edict laughed. "Now that makes sense!"

Eerey walked to the door above the wing and opened it. The bright yellow sun glinted off the glass of Eerey's dark goggles. The illusion of the mountain faded. All this gave Eerey a headache. The propellers spun slowly to a stop. The group looked at the ground far below.

"How do we get down?" Edict asked. "It's pretty far, but not enough for a parachute!" He pulled at his beard. "Which we do not have anyway."

Eerey looked at Edict. "Now you're glowing gold!"

Edict looked at his arm to see a sparking, golden sheen. He smiled. "Yeah. I look like a sparkler, but we have bigger things to deal with right now, Eerey. How do we get down?"

"Oh," Eerey said. "Sorry. I forgot to tell you we are on the roof of an invisible building. We can jump from here."

"Jump!?" Loofah said. "You might be able to see it, Eerey. Your keen vision helps you see in the dark and invisible things. All that the rest of us see is the ground way below!"

"Close your eyes," Edict said.

The orangutaur stamped his feet on the metal floor of the plane. "What! Do you really trust your cousin enough to leap before you look?"

"Too late for that," Edict sighed. "I've looked already. Eerey has never let me down, and yes, I trust her plenty to jump."

"Well, I don't!" Loofah said. "I'm not saying she's lying, I'm saying she could be wrong! Even if she sees an invisible building, it might not be strong enough to support our weight! What materials do they use in invisible buildings anyhow?"

"Well then," Eerey said, "let me be the first to jump. If I fall you'll know that it's not safe."

Eerey adjusted her backpack and stepped out onto the wing.

Loofah gulped as she leapt off. "No!" Loofah exclaimed.

After a few feet, Eerey struck a sold surface. She fell down on a flat, invisible surface. Standing to her feet, she brushed off the sleeves of her jumpsuit. "I guess that answers that question."

Loofah and Edict looked at each other and shrugged. At the same time, they jumped. Edict landed on the surface, while Loofah took a long leap with his powerful legs.

"Loofah-no!" Eerey shouted. It was too late. The orangutaur began falling, as he had leapt past the invisible edge.

Edict rushed to where Loofah fell, but Eerey grabbed his shoulder. "You can't see the edge, Edict!"

Eerey rushed to the edge and looked down. Loofah laid on his side about twenty feet below, suspended in the air. "Gaahh! That hurt!"

"Are you alright, Loofah?" Eerey asked.

Loofah shook his head. "I'm going to be sick!"

Eerey nodded and backed away. "We'll come down and get you!" She turned to Edict. "Where's Pen?"

Edict turned to look. Only a moth struggled in the wind and floated across the landscape. "I don't know! He was just standing there and now he's gone! He's going to trick us."

Eerey set her jaw. "No, he won't. Not if I can help it. First we have to rescue Loofah." She gestured. "Follow me."

Edict followed Eerey, cautiously stepping over the invisible roof. Far below, they saw green grass. Edict scratched his head. "Why is there grass under the building?"

Eerey shrugged. "They must not have built a ground floor. The grass would naturally grow with sunlight and moisture."

Edict nodded. "Yeah-but who are they?"

Eerey started down a set of tall, invisible stairs. The others followed, but cautiously. "I don't know," Eerey admitted, "but they must have been tall. The stairs are nearly three-feet tall, and the ceiling about thirty!" She nodded. "They were either tall or liked tall ceilings."

With invisible ceilings, the light did not diminish at all as they descended the stairs. "I can't see the stairs, Eerey," Edict reminded. "How far is it?"

Eerey shook her head. "The roof seemed about 50-yards-long, but I'm not very good at judging distance."

"Well," Edict said, "I can see Loofah from here. Let's get him!" He began to move toward his friend. "Ow!" Edict hand went to his nose. "There's a wall there!"

Eerey smiled. "That's why you should let me lead."

Edict frowned. "Lead on. McGuff."

Eerey moved cautiously, keeping Loofah in focus. "Loofah seems too scared to move," Eerey said. "His injured hoof probably hurts, I'd bet."

"What does it this invisible tower look like?" Edict asked.

Eerey shrugged. "Like a box. There doesn't seem to be any decorations or furniture. It's actually quite beautiful in a plain sort of way."

Edict remained silent as he followed her. Soon they tasted the cool air coming from the balcony. "No door here," Eerey remarked. "Step carefully."

Eerey stepped onto the balcony where Loofah waited. "Took you long enough!" he said.

"We can go," Eerey suggested.

Loofah's eyes widened. "No, no! Please, get me out of here!"

Eerey walked over to the orangutaur and took his injured hoof. "Ow!" Loofah said.

"Sorry," Eerey said. "I've got to examine it." Eerey carefully turned the ankle as Loofah gritted his teeth. She set the hoof down carefully. "Well, I don't think it's broken. Just sprained." She unzipped her bag and began rummaging inside. "We don't have any gauze to wrap it up, but Eightball can coat it with webbing. That should give you a type of cast." She brought Eightball out, his eight legs dangling. He growled as he looked at Loofah.

The orangutaur cringed. "No! Keep that thing away from me!"

Eerey sighed. "It'll give you a chance to follow us until we can get something to make a splint."

The orangutaur cringed. "I don't want it anywhere near me!"

"We could leave you here," Edict said.

Loofah closed his eyes. "Okay. Just do it."

"Just stay still, Loofah." Eerey sighed. She squeezed the belly of Eightball, adjusting Loofah's leg with her other arm. The spider released its webbing and coated Loofah's injured leg.

Eerey stopped and put the struggling spider back in the backpack. "Okay, Loofah. That should do it. This is just a quick fix. You'll have to walk as best as you can using three hooves until we find something to use for a splint."

Loofah opened his eyes. Spider webbing coated his ankle. He stood to test it. He grimaced at the pain as he tried to walk.

"How's it feel?" Edict asked.

"Not great," Loofah admitted, "but better. I can limp along with this."

Eerey looked at the ground far below. "Well then, let's move along."

Eerey returned to the building as the others followed. "Why are we following her?" Loofah asked.

"Because she can see the building and we can't," Edict replied. "If we get lost in here we could starve to death before we found our way out."

"Oh," Loofah replied.

They continued on through the building, taking the massive steps with caution. Edict held Loofah's arm and helped him down the stairs. "I don't know if I can do this," Loofah said as they reached a floor, "at least not without resting."

Eerey sighed and nodded. "I think we will all need a rest."

As she sat down, a loud noise like a slow, steady hammering resounded through the walls. "What was that?"

"I don't know," Edict replied. "I think we won't get to rest for long, though!"

Loofah looked about. "Can you see them Eerey?"

Eerey frantically looked about, seeking the origin of the sounds. "No."

"Why not?" Loofah asked. "I thought you could see invisible things?"

"I think they're invisible. I can't see invisible things through invisible walls!" Eerey said. "It makes it harder, at least!"

Should we run away?" Edict asked.

Eerey shook her head. "That wouldn't do much good. They can see us–if they are like us. I think they are very close from the sounds of it. We ought to wait it out. Maybe they didn't hear us. I don't know how we can hide from them."

"What if they have heard us?" Loofah asked.

Eerey shrugged. "In that case, we'd better hope they're friendly. We should be ready to run, whatever the case is."

Loofah looked down at his leg, wrapped in spider webbing. "I'm not gonna run very fast with this thing."

Eerey tried to discern where the sound came from. It continued steadily and grew louder. Suddenly, her eyes grew wide as she stared. "I guess it won't do any good for you to run anyway, Loofah." Her throat became dry. She wanted to scream. She wanted to run. She wanted to do anything, though she could only manage to say, "She's here. She's a giant."

CHAPTER VI

WHEREFORE MONSTRATOR

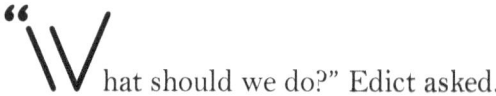hat should we do?" Edict asked.

"Stand still," Eerey said. "Don't make a move."

Edict shrugged. "It's not like we were planning on it. What's the giant look like?"

"Giant." Eerey said. Nobody contradicted her. She wasn't prepared to describe what she saw. The giant, or rather giantess, stood about fifteen feet tall. Her feminine features and graceful figure felt angelic to Eerey. The angular features of the face included a thin, sharp nose and thin mouth. Her ears were thin and pointed at the top. Her skin was olive brown. Her eyes were a deep, clear blue. Over a flowing, blue dress she wore a thin white robe that fluttered like a spider's web in the wind.

Eerey stepped toward the creature and whispered, "Hello."

Tilting her head to the side, the giantess seemed to smile-though the lipless mouth didn't change. "Hello." It said in a loud-but-gentle voice.

Eerey cleared her throat. "My name is Eerey." She said.

"Eerey," the giantess repeated. "Yes."

Eerey cleared her throat. "This is my cousin, Edict, and our friend, Loofah."

The creature nodded slightly. "Edict. Loofah. Yes."

Eerey smiled quizzically. "Who are you?"

The giantess straightened. "Who. Yes."

"Yes, who?" Edict asked. "Who are you talking to?"

Eerey laughed. "I am sorry. They cannot see you."

"See. Yes." The giantess grasped a shiny, silver ring on her finger and spun it around. As she turned the ring, she became visible.

Loofah and Edict stepped back and let out a sigh. Loofah said, "Ow!" as he realized he stepped on his injured leg. He sat down and grimaced.

Eerey didn't turn at the Orangutaur's exclamation. "Where are you from?"

The giant nodded. "From. Monstrator. Yes."

Eerey's eyes widened. "Monstrator? You mean the planet?"

The giant tilted her head in a curious manner. "Planet. Yes."

"Where's Monstrator?" Loofah asked.

Eerey sighed. "It's near the sun-nearer than Mercury, some think. Charles Fort claimed he discovered it but he wasn't taken seriously by the scientific community. On much of anything. To tell the truth, I didn't take it seriously either. I won't take it seriously until I have proof."

The giantess stood by patiently as Eerey spoke. "Proof. Yes."

"How did Charles Fort know it was called Monstrator?" Loofah asked.

Eerey shrugged. "Maybe he had some information." She turned back to the giantess. "What is your name?"

Blinking, the giantess replied, "Name. Yes."

Edict laughed. "Do you think she even understands?"

The giantess turned and walked away. They followed. "Wait!" Eerey said. "I want to talk to you!"

The giantess responded without turning around. "Talk. Yes."

Eerey frowned. "You're not making it easy to have a conversation."

The expected reply came. "Conversation. Yes."

Loofah rubbed his forehead. He felt a headache coming on. "Say something besides 'yes'! Please!"

The giantess halted and turned to them. "You sure have a lot of questions for me," she said. Loofah's eyes widened at the reply. "Perhaps you should explain yourself before requesting information. You have told me little of what are you doing here. You have said little about where you come from."

"I told you our names," Eerey said.

"Names are not who a person is," the giantess replied. "A name is the least part of me, as it says little about my person, what I think, or so forth." She waved her hand. Eerey thought she detected a slight annoyance in the impassive face. "For your benefit, however, I will tell you my name is Eridona."

"What!?" Eerey said. "That's my name!"

"See how little a name tells you about me? I am not you, and you are not me." The face of the giantess brightened. "My friends call me Idon."

Eerey sighed. "I'm sorry. Where I come from people identify each other with names, and not much else. I'd love to tell you more about us, yet we are in search of our friend, Guy. He may be in danger."

Idon nodded. "This city is abandoned. He is not here. I think I can help you."

"Who abandoned the city?" Eerey asked.

Idon turned and continued walking. "By Monstrians. I am here to see if we can re-Monstrate the colony."

Edict rubbed his chin. "What happened to the colonists?"

Idon shrugged. "Lots of things happened to them. It got too cold, too much oxygen, and the wildlife was too aggressive. They left an illusion of a treacherous mountain to keep enemies away."

"The Monstrians all left?" Loofah asked.

Idon continued walking. "Yes. They all left. They left many millennia ago. I am here to see if we can settle this city again. The humans have become very aggressive. That is an issue amongst many others issues. King Gyges has a ring like mine. He can use it to turn invisible. He can see through the illusion of the mountain. He sees the invisible tower. It shimmers for him like a diamond. He sees it, though he will not show others. He's coming with an army today."

"Why don't you leave?" Loofah asked.

Idon shook her head. "There are Monstrians weapons in the building. Should he find them the world would be at his mercy. He has little enough mercy from what we have observed."

"Surely you can defeat him with your weapons," Edict put in. "We have seen the horse-ship."

"The horsecraft you mention," Idon said, "The horsecraft is not a weapon. It is dangerous to travel in time, and it must be used very sparingly. The weapons in this tower are without power. They have rested unused for many centuries."

Edict shrugged. "If they don't work they won't work for Gyges either."

"The technology is old," Idon said. "We have forgotten how to use the weapons. There is a possibility King Gyges will figure out how to power them again. He cannot get his hands on them."

"You ought to hide them," Loofah said.

Idon shrugged. "I would like to. I cannot find them. They are invisible."

Loofah raised his eyebrows. "YOU are invisible! Can't you see them?"

"It is difficult to see invisible things through invisible walls," Idon replied. "Even Gyges will have great difficulty."

"Eerey can see invisible things!" Edict volunteered, oblivious to Eerey's leer. "She's the only one who could see Guy!"

Idon turned to Eerey. "You can see invisible things."

After a moment of hesitation, Eerey nodded. "Yes I can."

"You can help us find the weapons," Idon said.

"I might be able to help you," Eerey said. "It's hard for me to see through the walls as well, but I can be an extra pair of eyes." She looked over the dry plain. "I don't think we have much time anyway."

An army of about four dozen, two-wheeled chariots rolled over the plain toward them. Loofah gasped as he peered at the scene. "Orangutaurs!" Loofah huffed in amazement. The others looked at Loofah, then at the larger, armored, and muscled Orangutaurs pulling the chariots.

The wooden chariots covered with silvery plates of armor looked like chariots. The silvery-armored soldiers with red plumes of feathers coming from the tops of their helmets looked like soldiers. The scene looked much like an old movie, with one difference. Orangutaurs pulled the chariots instead of horses.

CHAPTER VII

GYGES' OFFENSIVE

"They're orangutaurs!" Loofah exclaimed. His lips broadened into a grin. "They're just like me!"

Idon shook her head and patted Loofah's with a sisterly gesture. "Perhaps they are not as much. Your heart is good. I can sense that from simple observation. I have seen great cruelty from the herd of Orangutaurs under Gyges command."

The lead chariot came forward to separate itself from the others. The orangutaur pulling it stood tall, its chest swelled with pride. It looked toward the group high above him and began to shout in a booming voice. "Tall angels in the tower!" he said. "I am Trunk, assistant to King Gyges! He demands you surrender yourselves and this tower at once!"

"Can he see us?" Edict asked.

"Of course," Eerey replied. "The building is invisible. We are not. Why can we hear him though?"

Idon leaned over to look at the Orangutaur, several floors below. "The construction material used in the tower is designed to allow light and sound to pass through." She stood up again at the end of the explanation.

"How is it solid then?" Edict asked.

Idon shrugged. "I am less than an engineer. It just is. It is not unlike a window, or a screen door."

Eerey looked down as the chariots began to move away from the tower. "What are they doing now?"

The chariots surrounded the tower some distance away and stopped. The chariot drivers began to notch arrows into their bows. "Can arrows get through the tower walls?" Loofah asked.

Idon shook her head. Arrows began to strike the lower walls. The shafts broke as the missiles bounced off the impenetrable and invisible barrier. A barrage of arrows continued unabated. Soon, an outline appeared of the base of the tower. Idon nodded. "I see. They are attempting to outline the tower for an attack. They are also looking for an opening."

Loofah asked, "Can they get in?"

"It is possible," Idon admitted. "The main concern when this tower was built was to keep out the larger animals. Elephants, 100-foot-tall camels, giraffes and so on. There are doors they may be able to open, though they'd have to wander around for a while before they found you."

"What do you mean?" Eerey asked.

"Well," Idon sighed, "I will go invisible again long before that happens."

Eerey's eyes widened. "You'd abandon us?"

"Of course," Idon replied. "You would do the same."

Eerey shrugged. "I doubt we would."

"I would," Loofah said. "In a heartbeat."

Eerey shook her head. "No you wouldn't."

Idon looked down at the soldiers seeking a way in. "A man as ruthless man King Gyges would be dangerous if he found the weapons. I would not wish to desert you. I must protect the innocent from a tyrant."

Eerey shrugged. "Friends don't leave their friends in danger if they can help it."

"You have only met me," Idon said. "We are not friends yet."

Eerey nodded. "Not yet. We probably wouldn't be if we left you in trouble at the first sight of it."

Idon nodded. "Trouble is coming," she assured and pointed to the soldiers. They carried large boxes from some of the chariots. Using piles of brush, they set fires at the four directions around the invisible tower.

"They can't burn it down, can they?" Eerey asked.

Idon shook her head. "Just watch."

The soldiers opened the boxes and moved away quickly. Gigantic spiders, about the length of footballs, began to crawl out and cover the ground. They crawled to the invisible tower and began climbing up the invisible walls. They skittered all over the tower, seeking for a way to escape the smoke.

Eerey backed away from the spiders, still many floors below. "They can't hurt us, can they?"

"These are giant spiders," Idon said. "Their sting is far more deadly than that of a scorpion." The giantess pointed. "They have found a way inside."

Far below, the party saw the spiders crawling about inside the invisible walls. In their frenzy, some skittered hard into the walls and disintegrated into a gooey paste.

"Giant spiders are not very durable when young," Idon said. "When they have aged a few centuries, they gain a hard shell. Few survive that long."

"Maybe that's why there aren't fossils of them," Eerey said.

"They are not our largest problem," Idon said. "The soldiers have found a way in."

Carefully avoiding the spiders and carrying a torch to ward off the insects when they came too near, a soldier walked through the opening where the spiders had entered. The spiders quickly began to spin webs on the unseen walls. The group watched in amazement as the webs spread over all the walls.

"Man," Edict said, "they spin webs fast!"

"They'll find a way up here," Idon said. "We should abandon this structure."

Eerey looked at the large, rectangular mass of spider webs far below the invisible floor. She turned to Idon. "You said you were concerned there were weapons in here they could use!"

Idon shrugged gracefully. "I have been looking for many days without success. You can see the invisible Eerey. Perhaps you can find them."

Eerey looked through the walls and floors. "I can't see anything invisible through the invisible walls," she admitted. The walls are more translucent to me than invisible."

Idon nodded. "If you find little, it is doubtful a group of soldiers and centaurs will find them."

"They're not centaurs," Loofah objected, "they're orangutaurs!"

Idon smiled lightly. "I apologize. I caused you to take umbrage. We cannot quibble over trivial matters. We must leave."

Eerey looked at the mass of cobwebs, the soldier in the building, the possibly deadly spiders, and the soldiers and Orangutaurs waiting outside the building. "How do we do that?"

Idon looked about at the soldiers below, the burning pyres and the dense smoke. "We must leave. That is enough. We must figure out how."

"I know!" Loofah said. "Those outside can't see us through the smoke. It is thick on the walls. We could go down to the room with the webs!"

Edict scrunched his nose. "Then what? Those spiders are probably deadly, and there's a soldier down there!"

Loofah looked at Edict. "We can avoid the spiders like that soldier did. I'm sure Eerey has a lighter in her bag."

"I do," Eerey said. "I have something better, though. I have Eightball!"

"How will that dumb spider help?" Edict asked.

Eerey set her backpack on the ground and unzipped it. With its legs wrapped about him, Eightball rolled his bowling-ball shaped and sized body out of the backpack. He deftly unfurled and leapt to stand on his eight legs. "The other spiders may respect or fear Eightball because he's older."

"Sure," Loofah replied. Dramatically, he dragged his hoof over the floor. "They might not respect me because I only have four legs."

Edict laughed. "I don't think they can count. Besides, you've got two arms and two ears. Add it up, and you're practically a spider!"

Looking down at the invisible floor, Eightball leapt onto the orangutaur's back. Loofah yelped. "Ah! Get it off me! Get it off!"

"Ah," Eerey said, "he's scared!"

Loofah stood still with the spider still standing on his back. "I'm not scared!" the orangutaur huffed. "I just don't like spiders jumping on my back!"

"Not you!" Eerey said. "Eightball! The invisible floor frightened him."

Loofah frantically reached behind him, but couldn't get a hold on the giant spider. He began bucking wildly. "Get him off my back!"

The others moved away to avoid the hooves as Loofah's bucking increased in intensity. "Whoa there, cowboy!" Edict said. "You almost hit me! I thought you weren't afraid."

"I'm not a cow!" Loofah shouted. "I'm more like a horseboy! And yeah, I'm scared! Help me!"

Loofah moved around, continuing to buck. "Watch out!" Eerey said. "You're headed for the stairs!"

Loofah set his front hooves down to stop. The hooves landed on the invisible stairs. He began tumbling head-over-hooves down them. Eightball dug into the Loofah's back to hold on.

"I'm going after him," Edict said as he headed to the stairs.

"You can't!" Eerey said. "You can't see the stairs!"

Edict shrugged as he felt the edge of the first step down. "I can't, but I can feel my way down." He put his hand against a wall and began to descend.

CHAPTER VIII

INTO THE SPIDER'S WEB

Thick smoke caused Edict to cough as he walked down the staircase. He couldn't see Eerey anymore. He supposed she couldn't see him either. He heard the sound of Loofah tumbling down the stairs. He didn't see Loofah. Edict knew that inhaling the smoke could knock him out, but he knew he had to help Loofah.

"Loofah!" Edict shouted before starting a coughing fit. He wiped the tears from his eyes. "Where are you?" He continued down the stairs, noticing he seemed to progress faster than he should.

The ground was quickly approaching with each step, almost as if he were parachuting down. He knew the steps did not cover that much distance. He shrugged off the notion.

"Loofah!" Edict called, careful to avoid another coughing fit. He saw the room full of spider webs below him and yet not much else. He walked toward it, calling Loofah's name once more.

"Here I am, Edict!" Loofah's voice replied.

Edict kept walking, carefully pushing aside a large tangle of webbing. He made out Loofah's figure through the webs and smoke. Loofah stood stock still with his back to Edict. "Loofah! Why are you just standing there?"

Loofah did not turn his head. "Can't you see?"

As Edict approached, he did see. Three enormous spiders, including Eightball, crawled around on Loofah's back. Loofah shuddered lightly. Eightball moved in a circle to keep his many eyes on the spiders. Eerey's pet hissed at the arachnids while they carefully looked for an opening.

"Get them off me, Edict!" Loofah said.

"Give me a sec, Loofah!" Edict replied. "I just got here!I haven't figured this out yet!"

"What to figure out!?" Loofah snapped back. "I've got three spiders crawling all over me! I'll tell you the sum total! 24 living spider legs are giving me a backrub! There are 6 fangs that could bite me!"

Edict nodded as he carefully approached Loofah. "Yeah, but there are only 4 fangs to worry about."

"How do you figure?"

"Eightball won't bite you. It looks to me like he's trying to protect you."

Loofah nodded slowly. "That's not all that comforting when one fang might kill me."

Edict shrugged. "We don't know that any of them are poisonous."

"I don't want to find out!" Loofah shouted.

"Stay calm, Loofah! You may find out if you get upset! You're upsetting the spiders."

"Oh, I'm upsetting the spiders! Don't you think they are upsetting me!?"

"Obviously they are. Losing control won't help."

"It can't hurt."

Edict nodded. "I think it might."

Loofah sighed. "Please, just get them off my back!"

Edict saw a smoldering torch lying on the floor. He sighed and walked over to pick it up. "Okay, just give me a second."

"Hurry up!"

Picking up the torch, Edict carried it to where Loofah stood. He blew on the tip, causing ashes to fly off it and reveal an orange ember beneath. "Alright," he said. "I'm going to touch one of the spiders with this torch."

Loofah closed his eyes and tensed. "Okay. Do it."

Edict touched one of the spiders. The spider squealed and jumped off Loofah's back. "That worked! It left!"

"Don't celebrate yet!" Loofah said. "You've got two more!"

"One," Edict corrected.

Loofah rolled his eyes. "Just shut up and do it!"

Edict sighed and touched the other spider with the torch.

"OW!" Loofah shrieked.

"Oh man!" Edict said. He batted the spider off of Loofah's back with the torch. "It bit you! Does it hurt?"

Loofah grimaced. "It hurts like the Dickens!"

Edict reached in his pocket and pulled out a rectangular tin. "I have some licorice lozenges in my pocket." He shrugged.

"Black licorice? How does that help?"

Edict put a lozenge in his mouth. "It helps me think."

Loofah huffed. "I don't have time for you to think! That could take forever!"

Edict's face lit up. "You know what? I think you're right! I should go ask Eerey. She won't have to think about it! She'll know already!"

With that, Edict returned to the staircase and felt his way against the invisible wall. He found himself going down instead of going up as he expected. He looked back, but the webs blocked his view from Loofah. He shrugged and continued walking down. The path ahead grew darker. As he continued, a pair of glowing, red eyes appeared in the gloom. The eyes moved toward him. He moved back up the stairs. "Loofah!" he shouted. "Something's after me! We should get out of here!"

Heavy footsteps resounded throughout the room, shaking the cobwebs. Edict came to where he'd left Loofah. Loofah looked at him. "I am having issues," Loofah's orangutan face appeared through the smoke. His orangutan-body and horse-body had split, and the orangutan rode on the back of the Shetland pony body.

"I can run," The pony said as he looked over his shoulder at the orangutan. "I need to get this monkey off my back. He's been riding me all day long."

"I'm not a monkey," the orangutan sneered. "You dumb mule."

Edict breathed out. "We've got to deal with this somewhere else! You can argue with yourselves later! Something's following me!"

A deep growl confirmed the statement. The orangutan rode the horse. The horse followed Edict, who turned to look at what followed them. The red eyes glowered through the spider webs, but he could not see the form.

"You led it right to us!" the orangutan said.

"I tried to run from it!" Edict said.

Loofah snorted. "By disguising yourself as a Roman Candle? You're a walking traffic signal!"

"Let's not play the blame game now! You know I can't stop sparkling! Can you run?" Edict asked.

The orangutan nodded, and the horse replied, "Like we've got a choice?"

CHAPTER IX

THE HORNS OF DILEMMA

The glowing eyes moved away from Edict, the orangutan on the pony's back. Apparently, it did not see them. They ran to the stairs and descended. Their pursuer snorted and turned to follow.

With the unseen creature pursuing, they found themselves at the dimly-lit bottom of the staircase. "There are stalagmites over here," Edict quietly said. "Let's hide behind them."

"But…" Loofah-the-orangutan began.

"Just trust me!" Edict whispered harshly.

The orangutan got off the horse's back and both of Loofah's

halves hid with Edict behind a cropping of stalagmites protruding from the floor. From their vantage point they watched a 9-foot-tall, bull-headed minotaur descend the stairs. It wore a tuxedo with tails, looking like some bizarre wedding crasher.

Loofah-the-orangutan whispered. "Aren't tuxedoes like," not that old?"

Edict nodded. "I don't know when they were invented. I'm pretty sure it wasn't before watches. It shouldn't be in this time period." Edict pulled at his beard. "Still, a nice tuxedo is a timeless look."

Loofah-the-horse snorted. "I don't care about his fashion choices. I'm just hoping he doesn't kill us. We can ask him later about his tailor."

Loofah-the-orangutan sneezed. He sneezed loudly. The minotaur grunted and turned its head to where they were hiding.

Edict looked at the orangutan. "Why'd you sneeze!?"

"I couldn't help it!" Loofah bristled. "Who knew I'd be allergic to horses!?"

"Don't blame this on me, Bonzo!" the horse said. "You're just jealous I'm a horse!"

"Jealous of you!? HAH! You're an four-legged candidate for the glue-factory!"

The horse's face fell. "They don't do that anymore!"

"I'm sorry," Loofah-orangutan said. "I didn't mean to hurt your feelings, pal. Seriously, we can't both be called 'Loofah.' It will just get confusing. What do you want to be called?"

"I want to be called 'Silver' if I have a choice."

"But, you're brown!"

The horse whinnied. "Whatever. Even a horse has its heroes. That's what I want."

"Okay," Loofah said. "I'll be Loofah then."

"Fine," Silver replied.

A shadow fell across their hiding place. The gigantic minotaur loomed over them as it looked on their conversation.

"What's it doing?" Loofah whispered.

"NOW you whisper?" Edict said.

Silver looked around. "I don't know about you guys, but I've got four good legs. I'm gonna use them!" The horse took off running at a gallop.

The minotaur chased after the horse with a roar. Its long strides easily outpaced Sliver and grabbed him by the back legs. It hoisted Silver into the air.

"Hey!" Loofah shouted. "Leave him alone!" The orangutan climbed up the minotaur's tuxedo and grasped onto its horns.

The minotaur dropped the horse. It fell crashing to the ground. Loofah held on as the minotaur vigorously shook its head to remove him. "Whoa!" Loofah shouted. "Take it easy!"

"No way!" the minotaur roared. "You tore my cumberbund when you climbed up. Now it's on!"

"You talk?" Silver asked as he tried to stand.

"Of course I can talk! I even have a name! It's Tor!" He continued shaking his head. Loofah still clung to the horns for dear life. "I can't tie my own bowtie! Talking's easy compared to that!"

Edict rushed over. "I can tie a bowtie!" he shouted. "I can show you how!"

Tor stopped shaking his head and looked at Edict.

Loofah held onto one horn, looking really dizzy. "I think I'm gonna be sick," the orangutan said.

"Really?" Tor asked.

"Yes," Loofah said, letting go of the horn and dropping to the ground.

"I wasn't talking to you monkey," Tor said.

Loofah bristled. "I'm an orangutan, thank you very much."

"Don't listen to him," Silver said. "He's a dumb monkey."

"Hey!" Loofah protested.

Tor ignored the remark and addressed Edict. "Can you really teach me to tie my bowtie? My girlfriend does it for me, but she's always jabbing me in the eye with her horns. She's a klutz."

"Your girlfriend has horns?" Silver asked.

The minotaur snorted. "All minotaurs have horns, even the girls! There wouldn't be much of point if we didn't-no pun intended. Now show me how to tie a bowtie!"

"Will you let us go?" Edict asked.

"Of course I'll let you go. I want you guys out of here! I was trying to chase you out! I hate time-tourists! They're always dropping their litter everywhere!"

Silver started to speak, but Edict shook his head. "Let's not carry this on. We're on a mission to find Guy. We can ask questions later."

The minotaur wiggled its ears. "Did you say Guy?" he asked.

Edict nodded. "I said Guy. Why?"

"I know of someone named Guy," the minotaur said. Maybe I can help."

"You can?" Silver asked.

"Of course, maybe I can!" the minotaur replied. "Guy was captured by King Gyges. He's probably in the fortress now."

"Fortress?" Edict said. "Where's that?"

"Across the desert," the minotaur replied, "but I know an easier way."

"What is that?" Loofah asked. "We should take the easier way. I'm not a desert animal."

"I can get you there through these caves," the minotaur said. "After you show me how to tie my bowtie."

CHAPTER X

MORLOCK REJOINDER

"That was too easy," Tor complained as they walked through the vast cavern. Grumbling, he adjusted his bowtie. Loofah and Edict carried torches to light the way.

"Yeah," Edict said, "but you made a deal to take us to Gyges's fortress. Live up to it."

Tor nodded. "I know. I didn't say I'd get you there alive. Or not bruised and bleeding. You might watch your mouth."

"Don't get us beat up Edict," Loofah said.

"Just so you know," Tor said, "that goes for you too monkey!"

"I'm not a monkey!"

Tor looked at Loofah. "If I say you're a monkey, you agree."

"Just for now," Loofah mumbled.

"Why could you get into the invisible tower?" Edict asked. "I thought it was impossible and impassible."

Tor stretched his powerful neck muscles. "The Monstrians built an access to the underground river." He nodded toward the wall where a small stream flowed. "The Monstrians don't remember it. An earthquake changed its course. That stream is what's left. We'll get into the fortress through a well."

"I wish I'd had time to tell Eerey," Edict said.

"You don't have time," Tor replied. "You need to get to your friend must be soon. Anything could happen while he's in the clutches of King Gyges. Besides, you would've had to go back through the webs. You might have run into a soldier."

"I just hope Eerey's safe," Silver said.

"I'm sure she'll be fine," Loofah replied. "She's always come out fine before."

Edict nodded. "Yes, but I'm worried about her too. Don't know if I trust Idon yet."

Loofah-orangutan looked at Tor. "I don't know if we can trust him either."

"You've got a choice," Tor said.

"What's that?" Loofah-horse said.

Tor smirked. "I was lying. You don't have a choice."

Edict saw something running between the stalagmites. "What's that?"

Tor stopped to look. "Where?"

Some more figures, hardly visible, ran past the formations. "Those!" Edict whispered harshly.

Tor's eyes widened. "Morlocks!"

"Morlocks!?" Edict said. "I'm a Morlock!"

Tor looked at Edict. "I took you for a troglodyte."

Edict bristled. "Don't call me that."

"I'm just saying you don't look like a Morlock," Tor said.

"I'm an honorary Morlock," Edict said.

Tor's eyes widened. "Is there any honor in being a Morlock?"

"Where I come from there is. The Morlocks are a proud race."

Tor shrugged. "It must have changed. I have not seen any good Morlocks down here."

"Maybe they haven't learned yet," Silver interjected. "It took humans a long time."

Loofah chuckled. "It'll take a long time for some humans."

Edict shrugged. "I'm proud to be a human!"

"You said you were a Morlock?" Tor said.

"I said I was an honorary Morlock! I'm human under my hair."

"Yeah," Loofah said, "and I'm an orangutan!"

Tor snorted. "So you said, monkey. I don't care about family histories. We've got to watch out for a Morlock attack."

A howl reverberated throughout the cave. More howls joined in, filling the air with frightening echoes.

Silver looked about with eyes wide. "I thought you said this was the easy way."

Tor's listened intently. "I said it would be easier," he shrugged, "but I've been wrong before. Nothing worthwhile is easy anyway. Look!"

In a distant cluster of stalagmites, glowing eyes appeared.

"Those are cool!" Silver said. "I like to collect rocks. I'm kind of a rocking horse."

"I meant look at the glowing eyes," Tor said. "They're Morlocks, and they're getting ready to attack!"

"That's not cool," Loofah said.

A Morlock stepped from behind a stalagmite.

"Can we talk about this?" Edict asked.

The Morlock waved his arms and grunted. The long hair on his arms flowed as a group of Morlocks joined him.

Edict sighed. "Okay then."

Loofah jumped onto Silver. The horse snorted. "Hey, get off my back!"

"We need a cavalry!" Loofah replied. "You can't ride on me."

"What is it with you two?" Tor asked.

"They're attached," Edict explained, "but there's no time to explain."

A wave of Morlocks rushed forward, grunting and howling. They crossed the distance quickly with great leaps. Tor, Loofah on Silver, and Edict all rushed forward.

"What are we going to do?" Edict asked.

Tor reached the line of Morlocks first. "Fight," he said. His head ducked low, he swept up three Morlocks between his horns and flung them into the air.

"Not how I wanted to spend the day," Edict said. He leapt to a grouping of stalagmites, pushing the Morlocks away as they tried to get at him. Edict's golden, sparkling glow lit up the cavern.

Loofah rushed into the fray, pushing aside the Morlocks with his orangutan arms. Silver kicked at Morlocks and guarded Loofah from any attacks from behind. "I wish we had some weapons!" Loofah said.

"I'm glad they don't!" Edict shouted.

"They can't use weapons," Tor said. "They don't know how. They can't tie bowties either."

"That's good," Loofah-horse said. "At least they can't have killer outfits!"

"Just don't let them get their hands on you!" Tor warned, sweeping aside more Morlocks with his horns.

"Now you tell me!" Edict shouted. "Help!"

Six Morlocks had captured Edict and were carrying him away. He tried to struggled, but their hands held on tightly to his legs and arms. All the Morlocks howled as they disappeared into the vast darkness.

"They're retreating!" Tor said.

"Yeah," Loofah replied, "and they've got Edict! We've got to get him back!"

Tor shook his head. "Trust me, you'll never find them."

"What will we do?" Silver asked.

"We'll go find your other friend," Tor said. "He's likely in as much danger. The Morlocks might think Edict's one of them and not hurt him. Guy is definitely not safe with King Gyges."

Silver whinnied as Loofah huffed. "That makes sense. They've accepted him before, and they wanted to take him rather than kill him. Everybody's in trouble now, maybe even Eerey."

The horse, orangutan, and Minotaur continued their journey.

CHAPTER XI

EEREY'S DILEMMA

The smoke from the fires filled the invisible tower. It caused Eerey to cough and tears to come from her eyes. "We've got to get out of here!" she said to Idon.

"It is all well," Idon suggested.

"Maybe for you," Eerey said as she tried not to choke. "I need to breath. What if those soldiers come up too?"

"The possibility has gone," Idon assured. "The stairs now lead downward."

"How did that happen?"

Idon waved her hand. "How is merely trivial. Only what is, is important."

"I imagine that's true. What is true is that I'm on my way to suffocation station!"

"You will be alright," Idon smiled. "You need to breath. I understand. I will return in a moment." The giantess walked out of the room.

"Wait!" Eerey shouted. She choked, causing a coughing fit. Her eyes watered as the invisible giantess disappeared from view. Eerey passed out from the smoke.

When Eerey awoke, Idon stood over her, gently shaking her shoulder. "Awaken young Eerey."

Idon held her hands out to Eerey. "Take it. Put it on. It will help you breath."

Eerey could not see what it was at first. She reached out to grab what looked like an Art Deco, horse-head shaped fishbowl. Metal contraptions and cords decorated its surface. Eerey coughed again. "What's this?"

"It was on the horse-shaped spaceship," Idon yawned. "It seems to be an apparatus for breathing in hostile environments. Those who used the horsecraft must have had a purpose for it, though it would not fit the heads of Monstrians."

Eerey coughed and wiped tears on her sleeve. She then placed the device over her head. Taking a deep breath, she smiled. The air was fresh and pure. "It works!"

"That is well," Idon said.

"Where is the spaceship?" Eerey asked. "I couldn't see it. I couldn't see you either when you left the room."

"I became intangible," Idon said. "The ship is intangible. I must be likewise to board it."

Eerey tried to scratch her head and encountered the glass surface of the helmet. "It's intangible? Mister Cryptic's wasn't intangible."

"It was at one point," Idon said. "This horsecraft can become solid as well. When it is parked, it is intangible."

"Why don't you make it tangible?" Eerey asked.

"It takes a great deal of energy to make something tangible or intangible. That is why seeing what you call spirits or angels is so difficult. They live on a different dimension and often have less energy and less interest to become solid or visible. Making your helmet solid again was difficult. Something the size of the ship takes much energy."

"Perhaps that is why Guy went intangible! He created a lot of energy making the submarine invisible. That's why he didn't just become solid again. He didn't have the energy!"

Idon smiled. "It is likely."

Eerey stood up. "Edict and Loofah aren't back yet! I must find out what happened to them all."

"It is safer to remain here," Idon said.

"Not for my cousin and my friends!" Eerey replied. "I must go find them."

Idon spread her hands. "Then you must go."

Eerey looked down at the room of webbing below. She turned her gaze at the soldiers amassed outside the tower. "How do I get through all that?"

"You will get past by becoming invisible."

"I can't do that," Eerey said. "I don't know how!"

"You can," Idon said as she grasped her hand and pulled the ring off her finger, "with this." She held it out for Eerey. "Use it wisely. You have seen what damage can come to you if its power is used to excess."

Eerey nodded as she took the ring from Idon. "I'll be careful," she assured.

Eerey went to the wall and began descending the staircase. It proved easier for her as she could see the invisible steps. Like Edict before her, she found herself descending faster than what appeared possible. Soon, she came to the room of webs. She turned the ring inward and turned invisible.

She walked through the webbing, careful not to disturb it and let the spiders feel the vibrations. She came to the ground floor and saw a soldier heading for the exit. His armor gleamed in the sunlight, the breastplate appearing like the suit of a lounge singer. Wearing a pair of dark glasses, he ran a comb through his black ducktail hairstyle before running it through his prominent sideburns.

"King Gyges," Eerey whispered to herself. "He looks like an Elvis impersonator. Plus, he's wearing my sunglasses Edict lost before we went to the Cryptoid ##! How did that happen?" Eerey shook her head and followed him to his chariot.

The orangutaur in charge of pulling the chariot sniffed the air as Eerey passed. "I smell something unusual, my King."

"That is so, Commander Trunk," Gyges replied. "The smoke of strange things burning inside the invisible tower, I suspect. Return to the fortress. Tomorrow we will return to conquer an empty tower none can see. After those inside have suffocated from the smoke. Every creature needs to breathe!" King Gyges laughed cruelly. "Our enemies will find an impenetrable fortress. They will fall when they move against me as they fall when I move against them!"

Eerey left the conversation and walked to a cart used to carry the sticks for the fires. She climbed inside as the soldiers began pulling away from the tower.

Eerey watched the cart driver goad the ox pulling it. She adjusted her helmet, which eliminated the smells of the wood and the dust from the road. She sat on the pile of sticks to settle in for a long ride. Her eyelids drooped and she fell asleep.

The cart rattled to a halt and caused her to wake up. She looked out to see the cart rested between the mud-brick walls of a fortress. She yawned and stretched before climbing out.

Between the fortifications moved a small community. Women walked about in various chores. One scolded a young child as another drew water from the well. A man sat at a merchant table selling vegetables and other sundry items.

Eerey continued in her observation of the people when a cart rolled through, pulled by two oxen. Soldiers guarded a heavily-chained young boy, looking disconsolate. Eerey held her hand to her mouth, forgetting about the horse-head, glass helmet she wore. "Guy!" she said allowed, forgetting her invisibility.

She saw Guy, the invisible boy. He no longer fit the description of invisible. His t-shirt bore the tell-tale picture of Claude Rains, the actor who played the invisible man in the first film in the 1930s.

She turned to move away, breathing a sigh of relief that no-one had heard her say Guy's name. She stole a smile. Guy was alive! The smile went away when she heard a voice. "I see you child," the man's voice said. She turned to see Gyges nodding at her. "I can see the invisible. I have spent much time invisible myself."

Eerey started to run from the King. He reached out with a lightning-fast motion and grabbed her. "You are to stand with respect and patience in the presence of royalty!" he hissed. "If you had not shouted your friend's name, I'd never have looked for you. Nice hat you are wearing too. I order you to turn visible and give me that helmet."

Eerey swallowed. "I can't," she said, "and I can't get the helmet off either."

Gyges spun her around to look at her. "Well," he said, "that being the case, I will need you. Your helmet proves that you are a pilot of a flying horse. You will show me how to operate the flying horse."

Eerey's voice quavered. "I'll only help you if you let my friend go first."

The King's eyes narrowed. "If you do not help me I may just kill your friend. I will not be held inferior to a little girl." He pulled at his beard. "Still, we can come to an understanding."

Eerey nodded. "What's that?"

The King's eyes lowered. "I won't kill your friend and you will show me how to operate the horsecraft."

"That's good," Eerey said, "but I think you can do even better. My friend won't be harmed and will be treated well, or I won't help you."

King Gyges set his jaw. "You drive a hard bargain, girl. I admire that. If you were visible I might make you my wife, yet a King needs a beautiful Queen to make his subjects jealous, not one they cannot see." He laughed. "Your friend is of no real consequence to me. If I am pleased by your showing me how to operate the horsecraft, I may even let him go free."

Eerey closed her eyes. She tried to keep from shaking. "I will show you how to operate the horsecraft. It may take some time to see if it is operational. Lead me to it."

King Gyges held tightly onto Eerey's arm. He pulled her along. "The horsecraft is secured in a room in my fortified dwellings. When you show me how to operate it my iron hand will rest heavily over all the countries of the world."

Eerey nodded. From what she'd seen the other horsecraft do and the undeveloped culture of the time, King Gyges could rule the world in a matter of hours. That would change all future history. Eerey gulped. It could even change the future enough to make it so she never existed in the first place!

King Gyges lead her into the square rock building. They passed through a chamber to a room with a heavy brass door. Gyges took out a key and placed it in the crude lock. The door opened slowly, groaning under its own weight.

Eerey peered into the room as Gyges lit a torch set in a wall sconce. "There it is," he said.

Eerey looked at the near-exact replica of Mister Cryptic's golden sarcophagus that glowed green and the copper sarcophagus that fired a red laser at the airplane. She realized she hadn't seen the one from which Idon retrieved the helmet. This was identical to the two she had seen, except the metal was black.

After a long moment of looking at the horsecraft, she ventured; "Why do you think I can make it operate?"

"Because," King Gyges said, "you wear a helmet like that of the giant flying this horsecraft. My great-grandfather found another some time ago that contained a deceased giant. An earthquake opened a crevasse in a cliff. My great-grandfather took his ring, thinking the horseship just a sarcophagus at the time. Another earthquake occurred and buried the horsecraft before he could examine it. My great-grandfather discovered the ring allowed him to turn invisible."

Gyges shrugged. "I think the giant in this horsecraft came looking for the other. I and my soldiers saw the craft land nearby. I gave orders to my soldiers to wait as I went aboard alone. I spoke to the giant and convinced him to go outside. The soldiers waylaid him at my command. Unfortunately, the giant died in the fight. We buried the giant and towed the horsecraft here discreetly."

Eerey wanted to ask if the giant had a ring. She thought better of it lest Gyges start to wonder if Eerey had a ring.

Gyges said, "You can get started now."

"Can I see my friend Guy first?"

"Yes. Right this way." This time, Gyges let Eerey follow without him holding onto her arm.

Gyges took Eerey to a different door. He opened it and led her downward into a dungeon area. She could see chains and cuffs hanging off the wall. The room smelled terribly and dust hung in the air.

Eerey halted on the stairs. "I will not work as long as you keep Guy in such conditions!"

"He has is uninjured," Gyges said. "You would do well to speak with respect that both of you might keep your lives."

"If you want your horsecraft you will move him to better quarters," Eerey said defiantly, though inside her fear churned her stomach.

Gyges shrugged. "Do you want to see him before he is moved to better accommodations?"

Eerey nodded. "Yes."

They continued down the stairs to see Guy sitting on a rock, his chin resting on his closed fist. He did not lift his head. The orangutaur named Trunk guarded him.

"Guy!" Eerey shouted. She rushed over to hug him.

He looked up bewilderedly as he felt arms around his neck. "What is this!?" he said. "Who's there?"

"It's me, Eerey!"

Guy touched the invisible arms that held him. He pulled the arms off, disentangling himself from Eerey's embrace. "Eerie? You certainly are, being invisible and all! Show yourself!"

Eerey let go of Guy and backed away. "Don't you remember me, Guy? I'm Eerey."

"We've established that," Guy replied. "Being invisible is a bit eerie as well as sorta creepy."

"You've got Claude Rains shirt on," Eerey said. "He was the invisible man!"

Guy waved it away and smiled. "That was a movie! People don't turn invisible!"

"I'm invisible!" Eerey protested with frustration.

"Yeah," Guy replied, "you're eerie too. I got it."

"Eerey is my name!"

Guy nodded. "What an odd name. It's a good description for an invisible girl too."

Eerey's face turned red. "It stands for Eridona Tocsin!"

Gyges shook his head in amusement. "I do not know of what you are attempting to convince your friend," he said, "he does not seem prepared to be convinced."

Eerey realized that Guy could be pretending so Gyges didn't find out he could turn invisible. Even if he weren't pretending, he could still be in danger if Gyges knew about Guy's invisible nature. She nodded her head. "I was just trying to get him to remember me." She shrugged. "I guess he's forgotten about me."

Gyges laughed. "Don't take it so hard, girl. He claimed he was confused when appeared here. Somehow, he had gotten into the room with the horsecraft. I found him locked inside and arrested him immediately."

"Can you please move him to a more comfortable area?" Eerey pleaded. "He obviously needs food and water too."

Gyges nodded. He turned to Trunk. "Move him to the empty room with the barred windows," he ordered. "Ensure his every comfort and his secure captivity."

Trunk nodded. "Your command is my will, oh illustrious King." The orangutaur saluted by lowering one hand and raising the other before repeating the motion in opposite.

Gyges turned to Eerey. "Come. I will show you around the fortress while you think about how to get the horsecraft operating."

Gyges and Eerey walked back to the horsecraft room. Eerey walked over to examine the ship. "I can concentrate better if I am left to examine the workings of this machine."

Gyges nodded. "Certainly. Work with haste. With the invisible tower and the horsecraft, I will be no longer a conqueror and king. I will be a god!"

Eerey bowed as King Gyges left. "You'll make a disappointing god," she mumbled. She let out a deep breath. Turning to the machine, she took off the helmet to let tears drain from her goggles. Guy didn't recall his invisibility and was a captive at the mercy of Gyges, who seemed to have little mercy to spare.

Her mind went to her cousin Edict and Loofah. What had happened to them? Why did they not return? It was too much to bear.

All of the answers depended on the horsecraft before her. She began touching it, attempting to figure it out. She felt for seams and controls in the black metal. Her genius mind began to unravel its mysteries. She stopped for a moment. "If I figure this out," she muttered, "it might change history and destroy everyone I've ever known." She couldn't move at the horrific thought. "If I do not, Gyges will probably kill everyone." She shuddered and began crying.

CHAPTER XII

AN ORANGUTAN TO THE RESCUE

"Well," said the minotaur as he looked up at the round hole above. "That is the well opening." He stood with the horse and the orangutan parts of Loofah in four-feet of running water.

"The well's too high!" the horse protested.

"Not for me," the minotaur said. "I can reach it. It's climbing up the dirt walls of the well that will be tricky. They'll weaken carrying all our weight."

"What is that again?" Loofah asked. "The well's walls will weaken with weight?"

"Cute," Tor said, rolling his eyes. "You go first, monkey."

"How will I get up there?" Loofah asked. He was immediately lifted into the air and thrown through the well. "Whoa!!!" he shouted, catching the rock-lined opening of the top of the well.

"Did you hear that?" a voice outside the well said.

"Thanks!" Loofah-orangutan whispered harshly. "That wasn't very stealthy!"

"You annoy me monkey," Tor replied lowly.

Silver nodded. "Yeah."

"There's an orangutaur child in the well!" another voice replied.

Loofah-orangutan crawled out of the well and hid behind it, keeping his body out of view as much as possible. "I'm okay!" he said to the women who voiced their concern. "I grabbed the rocks when I fell in! I didn't even hurt myself!"

"Are you sure?" the woman asked. "I can get the healer."

"I'm healed!" Loofah said, waving his arms. "No problems."

"Well," the woman said, "be careful when you play around the well."

Loofah nodded. "I will."

When the woman had moved on, Loofah went over to the edge of the well. "How are you two going to get up here?" he whispered as loudly as he could.

"Why would we go up?" Tor asked. "You'll do just fine!"

"NO!" Loofah said harshly. "I can't do this by myself!"

"What's wrong?" Silver asked. "Can't do anything without me around to carry you all the time?"

"You just shut your feedbag!" Loofah replied. "I'm the brains of this operation!"

"Worry about yourself, doc!" the horse said. "I wouldn't let you operate on me!"

Tor scratched his head. "What is it with you two? I don't get it.

You act like brothers."

"It's complicated," Silver said. "I'll explain when this is over."

Loofah snuck to the orangutaur stalls. The orangutaurs paid him little notice. He found a horse blanket and wrapped it around his waist. He figured it'd be okay unless anyone took a close look at his movements. He found a spot to sit down by the wall of a building and arranged the blanket to look like it covered four legs. He left his arms out to help in the disguise.

He heard a sharp whisper from behind him. "Hey you!"

Loofah turned to look. He saw a boy behind the barred window he sat beneath.

"Can you help me?" the boy asked.

"I probably can," Loofah said. "It depends on what you need and why you need it."

"I need you to find an invisible girl for me," the boy said, "and give her a message."

Loofah rolled over as some orangutaur soldiers passed. "Where would I find the girl if I did want to help you? You don't see invisible girls every day, you know."

"She should be somewhere in this building," the boy replied.

"What!" Loofah shouted. He looked about to see if anyone heard him. He lowered his voice. "You're in the building already. Why don't you look for her?"

"Because I'm locked in this room. Please help me."

Loofah sighed. "Alright. Who is she?"

"Her name is Eerey."

"Eerey!?" Loofah's eyes widened. "I know a girl named Eerey!"

"Really?" the boy asked. "How do you know her?"

Loofah puffed out his chest. "I helped her and her cousin escape a zoo and an underwater island."

"Loofah?" the boy asked.

"Yeah, I'm Loofah. What of it?"

"I'm Guy!" Guy said. "Remember me?"

"I remember Guy. You're not Guy," Loofah decided.

"How do you know?"

"Guy is invisible and you're not." Loofah stated his evidence emphatically.

"I was invisible when I was with you," Guy explained. "After the incident on the submarine I was teleported or something like that to this fortress."

Loofah's eyes widened. "How did you know about the submarine?"

"Because I'm Guy!"

"I already told you, Guy is invisible!"

"If I'm not Guy, you're not Loofah."

"How do you know?"

"Loofah is an orangutaur. You are an orangutan!"

"Yes," Loofah-orangutan agreed, "I was an orangutaur, but I'm not anymore."

"It's just like me, Loofah!" Guy replied. "I was invisible. I've changed."

Loofah stood and peered into the window. "Maybe you're lying. You could be Pen!"

Guy nodded. "I could be. Why would Pen be visible if he was imitating an invisible boy?"

"I don't know-why would Pen be visible if he was imitating an invisible boy?"

Guy breathed in. "It's not a riddle, you idiot! Pen wouldn't be invisible if he wanted to look like me. He doesn't know I'm visible!"

Loofah pulled at his beard. "That makes sense, I guess."

"Of course it does! You're Loofah, though you're not an orangutaur, and I'm Guy even though I'm visible!"

"Wait a minute!" Loofah said. "You said Eerey is invisible!"

"Well, she was the last time I saw her. I don't know if she still is invisible."

"Did you ask her why she was invisible?"

"I couldn't! King Gyges would know I used to be invisible and he might try to use that. I couldn't even let her know I recognized her, because King Gyges wanted her to do something and he would use that against her and me both!"

Loofah huffed. "Well, I guess I'll help. Just remember-I'm watching you! What does this King Gyges want with Eerey?"

Guy breathed a sigh of relief. "King Gyges wanted Eerey to work on a metal horse."

"A metal horse!" Loofah said loudly, before looking about him. A lady stopped and looked before continuing on her way.

"You've got to be quieter Loofah," Guy admonished. "This is dangerous business."

Loofah lowered his voice. "A metal horse like Mister Cryptic's sarcophagus?"

Guy shrugged. "I don't know what you're talking about. Just go find Eerey. Time is going fast!"

Loofah moved away cautiously. He saw the door to the square, mudbrick building. Orangutaurs and soldiers came and went. Moving to a place nearer the door, he waited until a moment when none were entering or exiting. He opened the door and snuck in.

Once inside, he found a place to hide and discarded the blanket. He moved about the large front chamber and listened at the many doors around it, hiding whenever necessary. He saw orangutaurs and soldiers on his way, but few paid much attention to him. "Gyges must feel pretty secure," he said quietly. "The security is pathetic."

He came to a door and listened at it. He heard the sounds of a girl sobbing. He tried the door, but it was locked with a large padlock under the knob. "It's locked!" he said quietly. He looked around the area and saw a rock sitting on the floor. "Maybe I can bust the lock with that rock. I really am missing Silver. Then talking to myself wouldn't look strange." Loofah shrugged and picked up the rock. There was a key underneath it. He picked it up. "I wonder?" He put the key in the padlock and turned it. The padlock opened easily. He looked at the rock. "Who's the idiot who thought that would work?"

Slowly, he turned the knob. He pushed the door open slowly, trying to stay quiet. Sliding into the room, he shut the door behind him.

The quiet sobbing continued, but there was nobody he could see in the room. "Eerey?" he whispered. "Is that you?"

Eerey turned around to see Loofah. "Loofah! What happened to you?"

"I was bit by a spider," he grumbled. "It made me split in two. I'm the better half."

Eerey wiped the tears from her goggles and put the helmet back on. "Are you okay? Does it hurt?"

"Yes and no," Loofah said. "Yes, I'm okay and no, it doesn't hurt. It actually feels good in a way, and like I'm missing two legs in another way."

"It's good that it doesn't hurt at least," Eerey said.

"What about you?" Loofah asked. "You're invisible!"

Eerey nodded. "Idon gave me a ring," she whispered. "I can't let King Gyges find out."

"Find out what?" Guy asked.

"Anything," Eerey said. "He's dangerous, and I'm afraid."

"What's he keeping you here for?" Loofah asked.

"To fix the horsecraft," Eerey replied.

Loofah noticed the metal horse machine. "Can you fix it?"

"I don't know," Eerey said. "I don't know if I want to, either. It could mean the end of the future if Gyges learns to use it!"

CHAPTER XIII

FOR FUTURE ENDS

Loofah pulled at his chin hair. "The end of the future? That sounds bad."

"I don't know if it is bad or not," Eerey said. "I just want my friends and I to stay alive. What are you doing here anyway?"

"Well, I came with my horse-half and Tor came to rescue Guy," Loofah said. "Tor's a minotaur."

"What about Edict?" Eerey asked. "Is he okay?"

"Oh yeah! I forgot to tell you!" Loofah said. "Edict was kidnapped by Morlocks and we couldn't find him."

Eerey's heart raced. "You couldn't find him? How hard did you look?"

Loofah shrugged. "We didn't look for him."

Eerey's jaw dropped. "Why didn't you look for him!?"

"Because Tor said it was impossible. He said the Morlocks were too good at hiding, and we should concentrate on saving Guy."

"Why are you listening to a minotaur you don't even know?"

"He seems smart. Even the horse agreed with him!"

"You are the horse!" Eerey reminded. "It's your other half!"

"Yeah, but I'm the better half. I thought I said that already."

Eerey held her head. "It doesn't matter. You can't trust Tor just because you think he's smart. You've got to get to know him or stay away from him. If he'll help you find Edict that'd be great."

Loofah scratched his head. "Okay. We'll search for Edict after we save Guy. Come on."

Eerey shook her invisible head. "No. I've got to stay here and figure out the horsecraft."

"I thought you said Gyges could use it to destroy the future."

Eerey nodded. "That is why I have to take it away from him. I can only do that if I figure out how to use it or destroy it. If I just leave, he might find a way to get it working."

"What do I do, then?"

"Go try to figure out a way to rescue Guy," Eerey said. "He might be able to help you find Edict."

Loofah nodded. "Okay. I'm sorry about Edict. He's my friend too. I'll do whatever it takes find him."

Eerey felt the tears well in her eyes again. "I know Loofah. This Tor might be an ally, but be careful of him until you can find out if you can trust him or not. He may have bad motives."

"I'll be careful," Loofah assured.

Twilight made the sky grey, leaving Loofah more ability to sneak about. Not seeing anyone inside the building, he looked out and walked out the door. He returned to the barred window where Guy was staying. "Hey, Guy!" Loofah said. "I'm here to get you out of here!"

"Did you find Eerey?" Guy asked.

Loofah nodded. "She doesn't want to go until she's messed up Gyges plans for the horsecraft."

Guy nodded. "Why didn't you let me out when you were in the building? It would've been easier."

"Don't start in on me!" Loofah whispered harshly. "I've been getting abused all day!"

Guy sighed. "You're right, Loofah. I'm sorry. We've just got to work together and not bicker."

Loofah crossed his arms. "That's what I've been saying all along."

Guy started to reply, but thought better of it.

"Were you gonna say something?" Loofah asked.

Guy shook his head. "No. Let's figure out how to get me out of here. How did you get to Eerey?"

Loofah shrugged. "I found the key to the room she was in."

"Where's the key?"

Loofah held his hand out and showed Guy a small, brass key. "I kept it."

Guy smiled. "Give it to me."

Loofah held onto the key. "What are you going to do?"

"I'm checking to see if it unlocks my door," Guy said.

Loofah giggled. "It won't! That would be dumb to have one key that opened everything!"

"Maybe that would be better," Guy said. "Just give me the key!"

Loofah reached through the bars and handed the key to Guy. "It won't workey you turkey," he snorted. He watched as Guy walked over to the door and put it in the lock.

Guy let out a laugh.

"It worked?"

Guy nodded as he turned the knob. "It sure did!"

"That's dumb!" Loofah laughed.

Guy shrugged. "Makes it harder to lose your keys. I'll see you in a minute. Meet me by the door."

"Just remember that you're not invisible anymore!"

Guy paused and looked at Loofah. "Oh yeah. I'll have to be careful, won't I?"

"Yes! Be careful and stealthy!"

"Okay." Guy mumbled as he walked out the door. "It was easy to be sneaky when I was invisible."

Guy walked into the hallway, but halted when he came to the large room of doors. Gyges was walking across to Eerey's room.

"Oh no! Gyges'll notice the key is gone," Guy thought.

Guy was right, but Gyges didn't react as he expected. Instead of seeing if Eerey was still there, he rushed out of the building shouting "Guards! Guards!"

Edict rushed over to the door and turned the handle. It turned and he went in. "Eerey!" he said. "It's me, Guy!"

"I can see you," Eerey said. "You must have escaped, but you can't let Gyges find you here!"

"Come with me, Eerey!"

"I can't! Go away!"

The sound of rushing hooves resounded outside. "The orangutaur guards!" Eerey exclaimed.

Guy backed toward the horsecraft as the door opened to reveal Gyges and two orangutaur guards.

"SEIZE HIM!" Gyges snarled.

The orangutaur guards looked at each other. One of them cleared his throat and walked toward Guy with a tape measure. "Why do you want his measurements, oh King?"

Trunk hit the other orangutaur on the metal breastplate. "Not 'size' him, Taylor; you idiot! The King said 'seize him!' Never use a tailor to do a soldier's job," he grumbled.

Taylor shrugged. "Sorry."

Trunk rushed to grab Guy, who moved to the horsecraft and put his hand against its surface. His eyes went wide as the hand went through the horsecraft. "Whoa!"

Trunk orangutaurs rushed at Guy, but the boy sank into the horsecraft and disappeared.

Gyges roared. "All of you get outside and find him! He is to be executed!" The orangutaurs rushed outside with Gyges striding behind them.

Guy stepped out of the horsecraft. "I like him, but he ain't too bright is he?"

Eerey shut the door. "How did you do that?"

"I don't know," Guy said, looking at the horsecraft. "I just became intangible again!"

"You can become intangible?" Eerey asked. "Can you walk through walls?"

"I don't know." Guy tried to walk through a wall and hit his nose hard. "Ow!" his nose was bleeding. "Why'd you tell me to walk through a wall?"

Eerey rolled her eyes. "I didn't. You could have felt the wall with your hand." She took a handkerchief out of her backpack and gave it to Guy.

"Why are you invisible?" he asked as he held the cloth to his nose.

"Because I got a ring from a giantess named Idon," Eerey replied. "Why were you intangible?"

"I don't know," he admitted. "I have a hunch, though." He walked to the horsecraft and tried to touch its surface. As before, his hand went through. "I'm not intangible-this is!"

Eerey walked over and petted the horse's nose. "Only to you!" she said. "That's amazing!"

Guy nodded. "And weird! What a great security system!"

They heard the sound of hooves again. "Quick!" Eerey said. "Get into the horsecraft!"

Guy did as she said. He disappeared into the ship as Gyges opened the door and ushered in the two orangutaurs. "Where is he!?" Gyges demanded angrily.

Eerey shrugged. "You know as much as I do. He came in and disappeared."

Gyges clenched his fists. "I'll kill him myself!"

"You have anger issues," Eerey said.

Gyges' face turned a deeper shade of red. "What the blast are 'anger issues' and what do they have to do with me!?"

Eerey looked away. "Nevermind."

"What was he doing here?" Gyges fumed. "I demand you tell me what he said! Why did he come to this room where the horsecraft is? Is he attempting to steal it!?"

"I don't know," Eerey said. "He's not like he was before."

"How was he before?" Gyges said. "Answer me!"

Eerey crossed her arms. "It's hard to explain. I don't know why he keeps coming to this room."

"Bah!" Gyges sneered and waved his hands. "I will never learn anything from you!"

"Look," Eerey said, "when I get this horsecraft running, you won't ever need to learn anything again. You can rule the world! King Gyges the all-powerful!"

Gyges gave a thin, closed-mouth grin. "You are right, of course." His eyes narrowed viciously. "Get that horsecraft running soon, or it won't only be your friend that dies."

Eerey gulped and turned to look at the horsecraft while Gyges and the orangutaur guards left the room. She closed her eyes and nodded. "I'll get it running alright Gyges. I'll try everything I can to get it working and you're not going to like it. We'll stop you!"

Guy came out from the horsecraft. "Now you're talking! You're talking to yourself, but you're talking!"

"I want to keep it that way," Eerey said. "It's do or die or win or lose or never have existed at all!"

CHAPTER XIV

WRITING IN PEN

"Help me fix the horsecraft," Eerey said.

Guy scratched his head. "How? I can't touch it!"

"I know. That's what makes you perfect. Until I can get inside I can't work on it much. There must be a way to open the door. Go inside and look for anything that might be a door handle or something."

"It's dark in there," Guy said. "Too dark to see anything!"

Eerey took off her backpack and rummaged through it. She brought out a winding flashlight and wound it to charge the battery. She turned it on and handed it to Guy. "Here, try this."

"You think I can take it with me?"

"You took your clothes and shoes with you the first time. A

flashlight shouldn't be too much of a problem."

Guy breathed deeply and looked at the horsecraft. "It's kinda creepy going in there."

"You have a flashlight at least," Eerey replied.

Guy nodded and took a step into the horsecraft. "It's working!" he said. "I can see in here!"

"Do you see a door of any kind?" Eerey asked.

"Yes," he replied. "There's a wheel like one of those on the doors of the submarine."

Eerey let the concept sink in. She didn't remember seeing a door in Mr. Cryptic's sarcophagus. "Where is it?" she asked.

"It's right under the horse's neck," Guy said, "but I can't touch it at all. I wonder why I'm intangible in here?"

"I don't know," Eerey said. "Come out and we can think about getting it open."

"Wait!" Guy exclaimed. "What's this?"

"What's what?" Eerey wanted to know.

"It's a envelope," Guy said. "It's addressed to you!"

"What!?"

"It says 'for Eerey Tocsin' on the outside. It's signed with 'Pen'."

"I don't care if it's written in charcoal," Eerey replied.

"That's not what I mean," Guy retorted. "The signature says 'Pen.'"

"PEN! Bring it out here!"

"I can't! I'm intangible!"

"Where is it at?"

"On the steering wheel," Guy said. "At least I think it's a steering wheel."

"What does it look like?" Eerey asked.

"It looks like a steering wheel of a ship." Guy replied. "Like the one on the submarine."

Eerey scratched her head. "That's weird." She shrugged. "I guess the Monstrians may have come up with the steering wheel!"

"Oh wow!" Guy stuck his head out through the wall of the horseship. "You have GOT to find a way in here, Eerey!"

"What did you see?"

"There is NO WAY you will believe me!" Guy said, rubbing his eyes. "I don't know that I believe it! This is the most amazing thing I've ever seen!"

CHAPTER XV

CONSPIRING COINCIDENCES

"How do I get in?" Eerey asked. "Can you open the door?"

"Let me check," Guy nodded and disappeared into the craft. After a moment of searching inside he shouted. "There's a keyhole!"

Eerey scrunched her eyes. "A keyhole? That's impossible!"

"Remember in the Cryptoid Zoo," Guy said, "when Loofah thought the door wasn't there so he could open it? You have a key-try it!"

Eerey looked at the key to the door. "That will never work!"

"Just try it!" Guy said. "If it doesn't work, we'll figure out something else."

Eerey nodded. "Okay. If it will get you to forget about the key, I'll try it. Where's the keyhole?"

"It's in the horse's left knee," Guy said.

Eerey looked at the left knee and saw a small keyhole. "I can't reach that!"

"Can you climb it?" Guy asked.

Eerey thought for a moment. "No," she said, "but I know someone who can. You stay here while I go find Loofah!"

"Good idea!" Guy said.

Eerey was careful walking out of the room. She shut the door behind her and walked between a pair of orangutaurs debating. "I still say it all happened in their head," one of them said.

The other shook his head. "No, no, no! Dream endings are dumb. The story doesn't indicate that! It all really happened!"

The other orangutaur laughed. "Talking animals? Get real!"

The other waved his hand. "You're just taking things too literally."

Rolling her eyes, Eerey slipped out the front door quietly and walked around the building. She saw Loofah sitting against the wall. He was using the horse blanket again to hide his legs. His eyes drooped as he tried to stay awake. "Loofah!" she whispered.

His eyes popped open. "Eerey! Where are you?"

"I'm right here Loofah. I need you to come back to the room where I'm being kept prisoner."

"If you're being kept prisoner there, why are you here?"

"Just come on Loofah!"

The orangutan sighed as he stood to follow, careful to carry his horse blanket with him.

They returned to the room and shut the door behind them. Eerey stood in front of the horsecraft and pointed at the left knee. "There's a keyhole in that knee, Loofah. I can't reach it. Can you climb up there and try this key?"

Loofah looked at the key. "Why, it's the key to the door! It won't work!"

Eerey nodded. "I know that. Guy thinks the key will work. We have to humor him."

"I never said it WILL work!" Guy said from inside the horse. "I said it MIGHT work!"

"Okay Guy," Eerey said in a patronizing voice. "It MIGHT work, and we'll try it." She motioned to Loofah to get going.

Loofah took the key and began to climb the leg of the horsecraft. "This is an easy climb, you know. It's only about eight feet."

"Yes," Eerey said. "An orangutan is better at climbing and hanging on. Just try the lock."

Loofah held on and tried the key. It turned with a click. "Whoa!" Loofah said as he leapt off his perch. The horse-head split at the neck. Hinges at the bottom folded down to reveal a set of stairs leading into the horsecraft.

Eerey's eyes widened. "I didn't expect that."

The door opened behind them and King Gyges walked in with the orangutaur guards. "I did," Gyges said.

Eerey shook her head. "I haven't figured out how it works yet! I need more time!"

"You can't always get what you need," Gyges lowered his head and smiled broadly at her, displaying a row of sharp teeth.

Eerey looked at the shark-like teeth. "Pen!"

The false Gyges clapped. "Good job figuring that out! It took you long enough!"

"You usually try to disguise yourself as somebody we can trust," Eerey said.

Pen waved the thought away with his hand. "No need to be predictable. You must be most wary of me."

"Why did you need me to figure out the horsecraft?"

Pen nodded his head toward the ship. "There's a message inside for you. I left it there, knowing you would find it. It explains everything. Go on now! Read the message!"

Eerey began climbing the stairs. "If you've already been in the horsecraft, you knew how to get in and use it. Why don't you just tell me? This really isn't necessary, Pen."

Pen laughed and clapped. "Oh, but it is necessary! You will see it is when you read the letter!"

CHAPTER XVI

TIME TRAVEL HAPPENS WHEN YOU LEAST EXPECT IT

Eerey walked into a very sparse room with a steering wheel as described by Guy and a tall chair, apparently designed for a giant. Guy pointed to the wall. Eerey looked at the word written there and stared at it. After a moment she slowly nodded.

Eerey took the plain envelope, brittle and aged as it was, and opened it. The paper of the envelope turned to dust and floated in the air as Eerey walked down the stairs with the opened envelope. She offered Pen a wry smile. "Thanks for thinking of me, Pen. I will read this later."

"What!?" Pen shouted. "NO! Read it now!"

Eerey shook her head. "I have never been given reason to trust you. You're just like the boy who cried wolf. I don't believe you anymore."

Pen lowered his eyes. "I travelled back in time to leave that message!"

Eerey shrugged. "I said I'd read it later. If you did travel back in time you probably set things up to go the way you wanted. My reading the letter would just be a part of your plan."

Pen gave an Elvis sneer. Then he smiled. "Maybe your act of not reading it is part of the plan."

Eerey laughed. "If you didn't want me to read it, you wouldn't have written it!"

"There is that," Pen grumbled. "You have a suspicious mind."

"Thanks in part to you," Eerey said. "You can take on many faces, Pen. All I can trust with you is that you're always after something. You're predictable that way."

"I'm not predictable!" the impersonator of the Elvis-impersonating King replied. "Maybe I told the truth!"

Eerey shrugged. "Any effective lie contains some truth or it's not effective. It's hard to tell what is true and what is isn't. I need to find out for myself."

"Well," the false Gyges stamped his sequined boot. "Go to it, Nancy Drew!"

"I will," Eerey replied. She walked into the horsecraft. "Come on Loofah!"

"Stop them!" Pen shouted. The orangutaurs rushed forward as Loofah bounded up the stairs. The stairs retracted before the guards could follow. The ship faded and disappeared, leaving the two orangutaurs and the doppelganger alone in the room.

Pen put his hands on his hips and sneered, flashing his sharp teeth.

"I hate that girl! That didn't go as well as I'd hoped," he said.

"How did you expect it to go?" Trunk the orangutaur asked.

"I expected it to go like I planned!" Pen roared. "I planned so carefully! What went wrong?"

Trunk shrugged. "You couldn't predict that girl?"

Pen shrugged. "If I can't," he said, "I don't think anyone can."

"You said you were this 'Pen' guy," Trunk said. "Who are you? What happened to King Gyges?"

Pen walked to Trunk and looked him in the eye. "I am King Gyges for all intents and purposes. I look like him, I act like him." He turned to the other orangutaur. "Who am I Taylor?" he asked.

"King Gyges," Taylor responded.

Pen nodded and turned again to Trunk. "That's right. I'm King Gyges. Everyone in this fortress obeys my command. You would do well to follow suit." He turned and took the burning torch from the wall. He and the two orangutaurs walked out of the room.

***

For Eerey, Guy, and Loofah events seemed different. After Eerey and Loofah stepped aboard the horsecraft, the stairs retracted.

"What's happening?" Guy asked.

"I don't know," Eerey admitted. She looked out one of the viewports on the side. Pen was talking to the orangutaurs. "I think we're invisible!"

"Wouldn't Pen think to check?" Loofah asked.

Eerey watched as Pen left with the orangutaurs. The lights from the horsecraft's round ports lit the room. "He's leaving, so I guess he didn't think we might just be invisible. He must not be able to see the lights from the horseship. Weird."

"He'll figure it out," Guy sighed and leaned against the wall. "Hey! I didn't go through it! I'm not intangible to the horsecraft anymore!"

Eerey looked around the horsecraft. "Well, we'll just have to figure it out before he does." She turned to Guy. "Why did you phase into the ship?"

Guy shrugged.

"There must be a reason," Eerey said. "You're the only one who can phase. You're different."

"Maybe something to do with this being made out of the Aunt Alice?" Loofah suggested.

Guy's eyes widened. "It is the Aunt Alice! At least, it was made from the Aunt Alice!"

Eerey nodded. "Okay. Who made it then, and why?"

Loofah shrugged. "Maybe when Guy turned it invisible it affected the ship. It sure was glowing before it turned invisible."

Eerey nodded. "Like Mister Cryptic's horsecraft! We ALL turned invisible with the ship!" She looked at Guy. "That's when Guy became intangible and disappeared!"

"It might answer why. Maybe I came here because I'm attached to the Aunt Alice." Guy rubbed his chin. "I guess the Monstrians might be who built this?"

Eerey shrugged. "Maybe. Idon didn't seem to know, but it's possible. For now, those questions don't need answering unless it can tell us how to operate the ship."

Guy rolled his shoulders and knelt down. "It seemed to react to my presence. Maybe I am the key." He placed his hands on the floor. "Maybe I can make it do something like I did with the submarine."

Loofah rolled his eyes. "We really don't know anything. We're just guessing."

"That's what science is," Eerey replied. "It's all guesswork at first. Now Guy's experimenting. There's got to be an easier way to make this thing work."

"I think the horsecraft is changing!" Guy said. "Touch a wall and help me!"

CHAPTER XVII

EDICT OF KING BENEDICT

Loofah and Eerey touched the wall below the words Aunt Alice. They concentrated for long moments with Guy to no apparent effect. Loofah sighed. "What's supposed to happen? I'm getting hungry!"

"I don't know what's supposed to happen," Guy admitted. "I feel hungry too! I even have a light buzzing in my head."

Loofah huffed. "That's what crazy feels like. Nothing's happening!"

Eerey looked out the viewport. She watched for any changes. "Wait! Something's happening!" As she watched, one of the bricks on the wall crumbled. A piece disappeared from the brick and appeared on the floor. "Stop concentrating!"

Guy and Loofah came to the viewport. "I don't see anything," Loofah said.

"Not now," Eerey replied, "but when we were concentrating I saw that brick crumble!"

Guy shrugged. "It could just be old."

"I saw it crumble," Eerey said. "I saw a piece fall, but so fast I couldn't see it."

"It sounds like we did move through time!" Guy said.

Loofah yawned. "It sounds like it, but I need proof."

"Look!" Guy pointed at the floor. The tiles broke away one-by-one and fell into darkness below. "What's going on? Is it an earthquake?"

"I don't know," Eerey said. "It's happening in normal time, though. I think we've stopped moving through time."

A hole appeared in the floor. A Morlock wearing an eyepatch over his left eye and an ornate robe crawled through the hole. The long, grey hair hanging off his arms indicated his age. He looked about before talking to the hole. "It's clear!" Eerey heard him shout. "Come on up!" Morlock soldiers began to crawl out of the newly-created hole in the floor.

Eerey brought her hands to her face. "Edict!? It's Edict!"

"That's not Edict!" Loofah said. "He's too old!"

Eerey searched the room. "Open the door!" she said.

Guy concentrated and the head of the horse opened again. "Hey, I think I'm getting the hang of this!"

Eerey rushed down the stairs. "Edict!" she shouted, tears in her eyes. "You're alright!"

The Morlock soldiers surrounded Edict, but moved away when he gestured with his right hand. Edict looked at Eerey as she threw her arms around him. He smiled "Eerey!"

Eerey let go of her hug and looked at her cousin. "What happened to you? You're older, and you're not sparking gold anymore!"

Edict touched his face. "Does it show? I stopped sparking when the Morlocks held me prisoner."

"You're looking good for your age!" Eerey said. "I'm glad you're not a firework anymore!"

Edict laughed. "I'm fifty, but I'm still a firecracker!"

"Fifty!?" Eerey said. "You were twelve when I last saw you!"

Edict nodded. "I was 12-years-old when you last remember seeing me, but that was a long time ago." He looked at a corner of the room. "So much has happened since then, cuz."

"What about Eightball?" Eerey asked.

He shrugged. "I don't know. You took him, or will take him. That's a long time ago for me. I can't tell you too much or it will ruin it. You made me promise anyway, or you will make me promise when that happens."

"What are you talking about?" Eerey asked. "I'd want you to tell me!"

Edict shook his head. "No. You wouldn't. Not yet."

She sighed. "Fine. Tell me what you've been doing."

"I was taken prisoner by the Morlocks. I taught them to talk. I started with simple words at first like 'yes', 'no', and 'ambidextrous'." He smiled before continuing. "It was like teaching children, but extremely intelligent children and fast learners. They made me their leader. You can call me King Benedict."

"'King' Benedict?" Eerey repeated with sarcasm. "You must have a high opinion of yourself."

Edict shook his head. "You would think I would. I've found that the title gives me more responsibility. When I treat others fairly is when I feel deserving of the title. The word 'King' would not mean anything to me without those whom I serve."

Eerey smiled. "I'm proud of you, Edict. You're not the same

annoying boy I grew up with."

"I'm not a boy at all," Edict said. "I'm a Morlock King. Quite a change, eh?"

"Yes," Eerey said. "You used to look up to me. It's a bit different with me looking up to you."

"I still look up to you Eerey," Edict said. "If it wasn't for you, I couldn't have learned to be a leader."

"I learned more from you than you know," Eerey said. "There's no time to gather membership cards for our mutual admiration society."

Edict nodded solemnly. "No. There is work to be done. Even with a time-machine, time is fleeting."

Eerey looked at the horsecraft. "Can you show us how to operate it?"

Edict shrugged. "I never learned. I was never very excited when you showed it to me, but you haven't done that yet. The Morlocks live a tough but happy existence. You know; the simple life. I have no regrets."

Eerey hung her head. "You mean you won't come back with us?"

Edict smiled. "I mean I can't Eerey. I love you and my friends, but I wouldn't give up my life for anything." He looked appreciatively at the Morlocks. "This is my new family."

Eerey looked at Edict as he tried to hold back tears. "When you do see me, tell me I have to stay," Edict said. "I'll want to go with you, but this is where I belong. Please promise me."

She closed her eyes and nodded. "I don't want you to stay." She smiled. "I'll miss you really bad, but I will try my hardest to do the right thing." She pushed a lock of hair away from her goggles. "What are you doing here now anyway?"

"We're here to rescue you from what's about to happen," Edict said. He shrugged. "If we can."

Eerey looked around the windowless room, illuminated only by the lighted ports of the horsecraft. "What's about to happen? Is it bad?"

A large *boom* sounded as the room quaked. The walls crumbled, revealing the copper horseship that attacked the airplane earlier.

"Who is in that horsecraft!?" Eerey asked.

Edict stood to his feet with his soldiers. "I think you know."

"Pen?" Eerey asked.

Edict looked at her. "Oh. You don't know then."

Eerey watched as the horseship opened. The Monstrian giantess named Idon stepped from the ship. She smiled at Eerey. She tilted her head to the side. "Hello Eridona. I can see how naïve I was when so young."

Eerey grabbed the folds of Edict's robe. "Is that...is that really me?" She could hardly form the question.

Edict nodded. "No. Not you. It is who you might become, and who you did become for the moment."

Eerey punched him in the arm. "Stop talking in circles! Is it me or not?"

Idon smiled as she opened her arms welcomingly. "That is for you to decide."

Eerey breathed deeply. "If you are here, then it's pretty clear what I decide." She took a step toward the giantess.

"Eerey," Guy said. "No!"

Eerey turned to Guy. "You think you know me well? You were invisible on the outside, Guy. I hide my thoughts away from the world. I am invisible in the inside." With that, Eerey turned and walked to Idon.

"Don't do this, Eerey," King Benedict pleaded. "This isn't you. Not yet."

Eerey smiled at her cousin. "You are wrong, Edict. Idon is me. She is what I desire. To become her is my destiny. I know that now."

Idon took Eerey's hands between her giant fingers. "When you were young, I failed to trust anyone one. Even you. Since I have grown, I have learned to trust us both."

Eerey nodded. "I am ready to go."

Edict, Loofah, and Guy rushed forward. King Benedict waved his arm to his Morlock soldiers. As they rushed forward, Idon held out her hand. A beam shot forth and froze King Benedict, Morlocks, the erstwhile invisible boy, and the orangutan in their tracks.

Eerey looked up at Idon. "Please don't."

Idon smiled again and led Eerey up the stairs of the horsecraft. "No harm will come to them. Remember, I am you."

Eerey looked at Idon. Though the features were very close, she hardly recognized herself.

CHAPTER XVIII

GIANT MIRRORS

Eerey walked onto the horsecraft with Idon. The control room was as sparsely decorated as the one she had left. "Where are we going?"

Idon sat in the tall chair. "We will not go where. We are going when, instead."

Eerey continued to stand. She felt no force of gravity pushing against her as she would on an airplane. The horsecraft lifted into the air in a blur of motion. Despite Eerey feeling no physical effects, her mind was trying to take everything in. She sat in a corner and looked around. Idon used the wheel to steer the ship, though she showed no expression of any kind on her face.

Eerey looked out a port window to see that the horsecraft now travelled through space. She stood and walked to the port. The Earth fell away beneath them. They headed toward the sun. Its light blinded Eerey's sensitive eyes. Even the dark goggles didn't help. "The light is intense!"

Idon nodded and offered her mirthless smile. "It is only temporary, Eridona. Close your eyes if you wish."

Eerey shook her head as she looked at the vast darkness, the glittering stars in the distance, and the planet Venus sliding past so near Eerey thought it possible to reach out and touch it. "I would go blind to see this beauty," she said.

Idon let out a kind of a laugh. "That will not be necessary. You will see as we travel."

"We're travelling through time as well as space," Eerey wondered, "couldn't we get there instantly?"

Idon nodded. "We could. Everything that gives energy takes energy. You can only receive the amount of energy you put in. To travel in time takes a large amount of energy. To go the distance between Earth and Monstrator would take an enormous amount of energy."

Eerey nodded. "I see."

"You really do." Idon said in her monotone voice.

"No," Eerey admitted. "I really don't."

Idon smiled vacantly and shrugged. "You are trying to understand. It is without shame. We travel using energy from the sun. We receive more energy as we approach the sun." The giantess pointed at the lower half of the sun. "There it is," she said. "That is Monstrator."

Eerey looked at the small world, shaped like a rubber ball stretched to a point on one end as it rolled through space. Eerey discovered the sun's light, brilliant as it was, ceased to hurt her eyes. She took off her dark goggles. "The light! It doesn't hurt my eyes!"

Idon nodded. "You are becoming intangible."

"Oh! It's so beautiful!" Eerey said.

"With intangible eyes you can see a broader spectrum of light. You can hear a broader spectrum of sound with new intangible ears."

"Is that why don't Monstrians burn up living so close to the sun? Are they all intangible?"

Idon nodded. "They are intangible. In the past the orbit of Monstrator moved increasingly closer to the sun. The scientists at that time discovered a ship floating in space. With their limited space travel they captured the ship with an energy beam. They studied the metal and found that the radiation from the metal could turn intangible and travel in time. They built a new ship from the metal."

Eerey's eyes widened. "That must have been the Aunt Alice!"

Idon nodded. "Yes. When it fell with the gorilla sailors to the deep the energy in the metal continued to build. It became intangible and floated out of the Earth's gravity. The scientists found it many millions of miles from Monstrator. They retrieved the wreck. The closer Monstrator approached the sun more energy could be captured. The scientist created an intangibility shield to protect the inhabitants. As we approach Monstrator we enter that field. They found a way to stabilize the orbit of the planet in a close orbit to the sun to utilize the energy."

"None of this is believable," Eerey said as she crossed her arms. "It's all too much of a coincidence!"

Idon gave a genuine laugh. "I said the same thing at your your age. The daily events taken for granted are unbelievable coincidences when you examine them closely."

Eerey softened. "I suppose that is true. It is just a lot to take in."

"It will become familiar," Idon replied.

"I'm not sure I'd like that," Eerey said. "It is the oddness of it all that makes it so beautiful. It's like we're angels!"

Idon shook her head. "Perhaps it is similar. We started as flesh-and-blood creatures. It is more akin to dreaming. That is all. An angel is a word to express that which is difficult to fully understand. I can show the science behind the Monstrians."

"Have you met angels?" Eerey asked.

"I will show you something amazing." Idon said. The horseship headed directly for the sun. A yellow and orange sunspot made a loop as they flew through it. Eerey saw all the colors in the loop. So many that she could not speak. The colors of the sun amazed her eyes. "Wow," she said. "It's overloading my senses."

"It will be temporary," Idon assured. "We are to return to Earth now. You will become tangible again. Your senses will come back soon."

CHAPTER XIX

WAR OF THE MORLOCKS

"I don't want to go back! Aren't we going to Monstrator?"

Idon shook her head. "It will be too much for you. We will take it a bit at a time."

Eerey nodded as they flew through space. "There's Venus," she said.

"Yes. Monstrians hardly notice it. The light from the sun bounces off the atmosphere. Monstrator is a nightless world. Venus is most visible in darkness."

Eerey nodded. "So, are you going to tell me how I become you? You know I'm sort of curious about that."

"I can tell you little," the giantess said. "I recall only so much of the events that led you, I, us, to this point in time."

"Start with what you remember."

"That is why we are returning to Earth. Actions must be performed in the past to make this conversation possible now."

The horsecraft flew toward the orb of Earth. The pain of the sunlight once again hurt Eerey's eyes. The land and oceans became clear enough for Eerey to identify the continents of Europe and Africa. The horsecraft headed for the ocean Middle East. Soon, they followed a bomber.

"That's our bomber!" Eerey said.

"Yes. We must help keep it from crashing. We must survive."

In a replay that made Eerey feel strange, the beam fired from the horsecraft. It struck the bomber she was simultaneously in while being in the horsecraft. The beam formed a bubble around the aircraft.

"There are three of us here at the same time!" Eerey said. "I'm on the plane, I'm here talking to myself, and you're flying the horsecraft!"

"It's more than that," Idon said. "Every moment we are changing. We are less exactly the same as we were the moment before. Only when travelling will we remain the same."

"What do you mean?"

"Say you are driving in a car. You are affected only by what is inside the car. You can see things outside the car. Parked cars seem to move by quickly as you pass them, though they are not moving at all."

Eerey nodded. "I guess so. It seems more complicated."

"It seems that way," Idon agreed. "It is less complicated than it appears. Desert frogs can sleep for some time during a drought. They awaken when it rains."

"Is Mister Cryptic just asleep then?"

Idon nodded. "He is sleeping in a way."

"Why did the others not want me to go with you?" Eerey wondered. "You don't seem to be bad."

"You know me better than anyone," Idon said. "If you have difficulty answering that question for me, I am without hope to answer it for you."

"You are me!" Eerey said. "We are the same!"

Idon nodded. "I have experiences that you are different. You have memories of youth I have forgotten. I hardly think we are exactly the same."

"I will become you."

"Only if that is what you wish," Idon said. "Is that what you want?" It was the first time Eerey heard Idon ask a question.

Eerey thought about the question for a moment. "What would I gain from that?"

Idon shrugged. "A lifetime of experiences in an instant."

"I like experience," Eerey said. "I have a lifetime to experiences to come. I don't think I want to leapfrog over them."

"Some experiences hurt. Some are bad."

"I know. I wouldn't change the bad experiences I've had. They made me who I am today, and might make me who I will be. I am happy with who I am."

"Will you be happy with who you will be?"

"I don't know."

"You can find out. Right now."

"I can find out later too. No need to rush, knowing I will get there anyway."

"Perhaps you will not," Idon said.

"You know," Eerey replied, "you're starting to annoy me."

Idon sighed. "That has always been my problem. You never trusted myself. I was always suspicious."

"I think you're reading into it too much. What are you anyway, my conscience? You don't look like Jiminy Cricket."

Idon turned away. "Let us move on. We must go help Edict in his battle."

"What!?" Eerey exclaimed. "What battle!?"

"The battle between the Morlock army and the army of Pen in his disguise as King Gyges."

"Edict survives that battle," Eerey said. "I saw him when you picked me up."

Idon shook her head. "Your understanding is limited. All events are fluid until they are frozen. What you saw was one possibility. It can still be changed."

Eerey nodded. "Okay. How do we freeze it so it does not change?"

"We help Edict win the battle," Idon replied. "That is your future."

"It's happened already," Eerey said. "I talked to Edict!"

"Time travel is full of paradoxes. The battle is in your future."

"Do we use the horsecraft?" Eerey asked.

Idon shook her head. "That will disrupt the flow of time. The horsecraft is most safely used for conveyance only. Such power is difficult to control. These matters must be dealt with in ordinary ways."

Eerey nodded. She watched out the window. The horsecraft approached the fortress of King Gyges as twilight fell. Morlocks crawled out of the well and rushed over the ground toward a row of chariots pulled by powerful orangutaurs. The soldiers slashed at the Morlocks, who easily evaded and attacked the men. Eerey saw a young Edict directing the attack. "They cannot sense us," Idon assured.

Eerey saw a soldier attack Edict. Edict used his staff to try and ward off the sword blow, yet the razor-sharp tip sliced his arm. Edict backed away as the soldier pressed him. "Get us down there now!" Eerey said. "Edict's hurt!"

Idon shook her head. "You always rush to the rescue of everyone else. You fail to help yourself."

"Just land!" Eerey demanded. "There's no time!"

Idon guided the horsecraft to the ground. "You know Edict will be okay. You saw him as an old man."

"You said that could change."

"It can," Idon admitted as she landed the craft. "Your involvement could change it for the worse." The stairs opened.

Eerey hesitated, seeing Edict unconscious twenty feet away from the ship. "I never thought of that."

"Travelling through time means you can change things. It remains a question if you can change things for better or for worse. It is difficult to know."

Eerey clenched her teeth. "I can see Edict's in trouble. That is all I need to know." She stepped off the bottom stair. She became visible and tangible in the center of dangerous chaos. Soldiers ran between moving chariots. Morlocks leapt and grappled with the soldiers. The soldiers struck the Morlocks down with their swords. Morlocks overtook the soldiers by leaping on the chariots and knocking them out. The soldiers in chariots struck the Morlocks, though their agility allowed them to evade.

Taking a deep breath, Eerey plunged into the battle. She rushed toward Edict as she avoided the various fights. The soldiers ignored the unarmed girl.

Striking the soldier on the temple with his staff, Edict turned to see Eerey rushing toward him. "Eerey!" he shouted. The soldier stood to his feet. His sword cut Edict across his face.

"Edict!" Eerey shouted. She did not see the chariot rushing at her until it was upon her. She turned to the flashing blade of King Gyges as he swung the flat of his blade at her head. It connected, hitting her with blunt force. In another moment, she saw only darkness.

"Eerey!" Edict gritted his teeth and swung his staff at the false

King Gyges as he attempted to turn his chariot around. The staff struck King Gyges and sent him to the ground, bleeding from the mouth.

Trunk, the orangutaur pulling the chariot lost control and flipped it over. Trunk turned to see Edict.

Edict and Trunk stared at each other for a moment. Trunk looked knowingly at the unconscious impersonator of King Gyges. The orangutaur nodded to Edict and returned to the battle. Edict moved his gaze to Eerey and rushed over to help her. He pulled Eerey under the overturned chariot.

"Eerey!" Edict shouted as he shook her by the shoulders. "Eerey! Wake up cuz!"

Eerey opened her eyes and looked at Edict. "Edict?" She touched his bleeding cheek. "What happened?"

"It's the middle of the battle, cuz!" Edict said. "I'll be fine, but I can't worry about you!"

"I can take care of myself!" Eerey protested.

Edict nodded. "I know you can. You've asked me to trust you in the past. Now, I'm asking you to trust me. Let me do this alone. It's something I've got to do. This is my battle. Mine and the Morlocks. Don't ask me to leave it. I can't go home with you until this is finished."

Eerey remembered what King Benedict said to her in the future. The future might change depending on what she did. She gulped. "Of course I won't make you go, Edict." She smiled. "I'm just watching out for you."

"It's time you watch out for yourself, Eerey," Edict said. "You don't have to take care of everyone. I love that you want to help, but you need to take care of yourself too."

Eerey looked into her cousins eyes. "Stay here Edict. Follow your heart."

Edict hugged Eerey. "You too, cuz. I love you." Edict straightened his collar and returned to the battle.

Eerey hugged him back. "I'm not your cuz. I'm your sister. Whether by blood or not." Letting go of Edict, she looked and saw Idon's invisible horsecraft waiting for her. She looked both ways before running across the ground and up the waiting stairs. Once inside, she turned to Idon. "That is finished."

Idon looked out the eyeports of the horsecraft. "Edict has not won yet."

Eerey looked down to see Edict grappling with a soldier. "Yes he has," she said.

"Then we will continue to the next time repair." Idon turned the wheel. Events changed around the horsecraft, the battle played out so quickly it proved impossible to identify the victors.

"Why are we fixing things?" Eerey asked.

"The timeline is in a tumult," Idon replied. "Pen figured out the time machine. His travels are disrupting everything. It is dangerously close to destroying everything."

"We should take Pen out before fixing things," Eerey said.

Idon nodded. "You have removed him effectively by taking the horsecraft. He did much damage by taking on the form of the Monstrian giant. Now, we must repair the broken and tangled threads of fate."

Eerey rolled her eyes. "Sounds dramatic."

Idon didn't seem to hear the sarcasm in Eerey's voice. "Yes. Every change in the stream of time changes all those that follow. It even puts your own existence at risk."

Eerey nodded. "I know that already."

"It is good to know." Idon looked out the right side viewport. "It seems there is danger already."

Eerey followed Idon's gaze to see the black horsecraft headed for them. It fired a beam that struck the ship and created an envelope of blue light around them.

"Is it Guy?" Eerey asked hopefully.

The bubble began to constrict around Idon's horsecraft. "I do not think so."

The bubble pressed against the sides as the air in the ship became oppressive. Eerey adjusted her goggles. "What's it doing?"

"It is crushing the ship in a bubble of time energy." Idon said matter-of-factly.

Eerey looked at Idon. "What will that do to us?"

"It will be our undoing," Idon replied. "We will be undone."

Eerey looked at the black horsecraft, helpless against the inevitable fate with which it presented them.

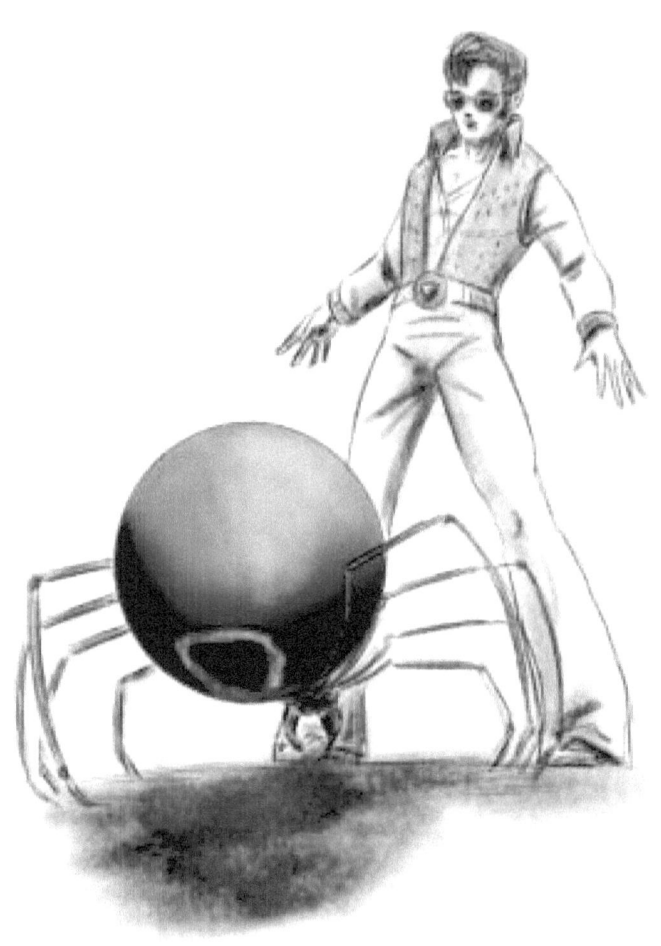

CHAPTER XX

TIME CRUNCH

Eerey grasped the hem of Idon's dress. "How can we stop it from crushing us!?"

"The way to do that is obvious," Idon replied. "We let it crush us."

Eerey furrowed her brow. "WHAT!? I've never been much afraid of death-but to never have existed at all!"

Idon nodded sagely. "Yes. If we never existed there is no reason for this event to occur. No one can attempt to destroy a person who never existed."

Eerey let go of Idon's dress. "I suppose that is true. That would be a paradox to destroy what never existed!"

Idon nodded. "You begin to understand. In destroying that which does not exist you inadvertently create it."

"That is nonsense," Eerey said, "yet it rings true. Still, I don't feel like being crushed before lunchtime. Until I don't exist, I will believe something can be done."

"You would like to do something to keep from being crushed. I think I understand why."

"Yes!" Eerey shivered as the metal let out a groan. "This is worse than pressure on the submarine!"

"Except that the ship will just cease existing. We will take action." Idon pulled at the wheel of the horsecraft. The metal groaned even more, but the black horsecraft strained to keep Idon's ship under control.

"Wait a minute," Eerey said. "If we can be in two places at once, like when we rescued the airplane using this horsecraft, there are more of us out there. Destroying us would leave them! Only we would cease to exist!"

Idon's eyes widened as she stood up. "That's right! There paradox would cease to exist! We are the paradox!"

Eerey smiled lightly. "You're getting excited, Idon. It doesn't become you."

Idon breathed in and sat back in her chair. Her impassive smile returned. "Sorry."

"Good. I can freak out enough for both of us. We have to remain calm and concentrate on the problem." Eerey pulled at a lock of hair. "Hey-what would happen if we fired at that horsecraft with a time-beam or whatever it is?"

"I'm not sure," Idon admitted. "It could kill us."

Eerey shrugged. "I'm willing to risk death over non-existence. Give it a try."

Idon touched the wheel. A beam of energy shot out, slipping through the shrinking bubble. It put a bubble around the other horsecraft. "Well," Eerey said, "that's a start anyway. Can you shoot the beam inside the other horsecraft?"

"I can," Idon said.

"If you can have the bubble expand," Eerey explained, "you can push it apart. It seems to me the Aunt Alice had trouble when the giant squid tried to open it like a clam. It could withstand pressure, but it had more difficulty when something tried to pull it apart."

"I will try." Idon adjusted the knobs on the steering wheel. The beam retracted from the other ship for a moment. Then it shot out again and stabbed through the hull. The inside ports glowed red as Idon adjusted the beam. The red light escaped through the splits that appeared in the seams. Eerey saw a figure moving inside as the glow lit up the horsecraft. She recognized the figurre as Guy.

"OH!" Eerey exclaimed. "Stop it! Turn it off!"

"I understand little," Idon said as she turned off the beam.

The ports on the other ship went dark as Eerey watched Guy fade from view. He was older than the last time Eerey saw him, perhaps in his twenties. He wore the same shirt with the picture of Claude Rains. "Guy's controlling the other horsecraft!"

Idon turned to look at Eerey. "There is a reason he would attempt to destroy us."

Eerey shrugged. "I can't think of one. Is there any way to talk with him?"

"There is more than one way."

"I mean a convenient way? Can you have the ship hover?"

Idon nodded. The ship stopped moving. The other horsecraft did likewise.

Eerey went to the window and waved her arms. "Guy! Why are you doing this?"

The lights on the other ship turned on. The pressure inside lessened as Guy came to the port. He cupped his ear with his to indicate he couldn't hear.

Eerey turned to Idon. "I don't know sign language, Idon, and I've never been good at charades. Can I talk to him?"

Idon nodded. "You may speak to him now."

Eerey returned to the port. "Guy, can you hear me?"

Eerey moved back as his voice startled her. "Yes Eerey. I can hear you. Cam you hear me?"

Eerey nodded. "Why are you trying to destroy our ship?"

"I'm trying to stop the damage you are doing," Guy replied. "You are crushing flowers in time's garden."

"Are you going to recite poetry to me?" Eerey asked. "I don't know what you're talking about!"

Guy nodded. "I didn't see you were with Idon. It must be earlier than I thought."

Eerey shook her head. "I don't understand. Idon and I are the same!"

Guy shook his head. "Idon is who you might become if this is allowed to continue. Did you happen to look at the world before you left us the day you met King Benedict?"

Eerey shook her head. "No."

Guy sighed. "Perhaps you should look below you."

Eerey peered out the viewport. Many miles of black rubble covered the ground. It smoked and flamed. Buildings lay awkwardly against the yellow skyline amidst piles of cindered bricks. People wandered in a daze across the devastated land. Their clothes were tattered. They looked hungry, fighting with bare hands over any scraps of food. It was too far away to see much, but what Eerey saw was too much. She looked at Guy, with a tear in her eye. "How did this happen?"

Guy shrugged. "Idon's travelling through time to repair things has left time in a tangled mess. It must stop, but she will not listen to reason."

Idon turned her head toward Eerey. Her expression remained impassive. "I will listen to reason."

"Have you looked outside, Idon!?" Eerey asked. "The world's a mess!"

"My involvement is to repair the damage." Idon said. She placed her hands on the wheel.

"You aren't me!" Eerey shouted. "You can't be!"

Idon smiled. "I am you. I am what you will become."

"You are what I MAY become! You said yourself that things can be changed!"

Idon stood up. "It can be changed," she agreed. "It is possible you wish to become me. You saw the beauty of the sun. You felt the freedom of intangibility. It is difficult to believe that you would settle for less."

Eerey set her jaw as she removed her goggles. "Oh, Idon. What happened to you? How did I get so lost? I have seen beauty, Idon. Yes, the sun is dazzling and beautiful. Even you are beautiful. So many things you have shown me are beautiful."

Eerey sighed and continued. "For all those things you've shown me, you seem to have missed the point of beauty. If you cannot look at the simple beauty of a blade of grass, the beauty of a rose is lessened. The beauty of the sun is nothing if you cannot appreciate a smile from one who loves you. When you seek so hard for beauty you can travel to the sun and still not be satisfied, perhaps you need to go back to basics. I hope is it not necessary to say more."

"It is less than necessary," Idon replied. Eerey looked at the giantess. Tears flowed down her face. "Oh Eerey, how I wish I could return to where you are!"

Eerey shook her head. "I have to grow much more. I am glad to be in this moment, but I've got to move forward."

Eerey held her hand out to Idon. As Idon took the hand, a blinding flash of white light filled the room. As it dispersed, Idon appeared at half her previous height. Eerey was not around.

Idon went to the viewport.

CHAPTER XXI

SYNTHESIS AND ANTI-THESIS

"Idon!" Guy hissed. "What have you done with Eerey?"

Idon smiled. "I am Eerey. I always have been. I joined my younger self to my older self or vice versa. We are now one."

Guy backed away as Pen suddenly appeared behind Idon. Guy said. "Idon, watch out behind you!"

Idon turned as Pen put his hands on her shoulders. A flashing of blinding light lit up the viewports. "NO!" Guy howled. Idon was gone. Pen appeared in her place, wearing a giant-sized Gyges guise. A broad, shark-toothed smile grew on his Elvis-impersonating, sneering lips.

"Oh yes, Guy," Pen replied. "Eerey never even suspected. I never even suspected myself at first. That little brat and I are one!"

"But how?" Guy's heart sunk.

"All of us have a dark side, Guy." Pen laughed. "Eerey never thought to check."

"But…I've seen you both apart." Guy said.

Pen nodded. "As have I. It wasn't until I came here and started travelling around in time that I learned the truth. Eerey and I were destined to meet." Pen lowered his eyes. "We we destined to fight. Years ago, I turned into a worm. I then split and became many different creatures. One was Eerey, one was I. Unfortunately, none of us could remember. A worm's brain is not given to having a good memory. I do not even remember anything from before that event. It is only through investigation that I found out that much."

"Eerey's a kind person," Guy argued. "You can't be a part of her! She hates the dark. You do not."

"She hates the dark because she is afraid that something frightful and evil is in it." Pen looked at the floor. "She was very right to be afraid. She is that evil thing haunting the shadows. Or at least, part of her is."

Guy resigned himself to the truth. "That part is you."

Pen nodded. "After all, my middle name is Umbra."

"Umbra?" Guy quizzed.

"It means 'dark shadow' or somesuch in Latin."

"What does Eerey mean?" Guy asked.

"I do not know. It is odd that she pronounces it 'ear-ee' when it should be pronounced 'ear-ray' as in a ray of light." Pen shrugged. "It's only a nickname anyway."

Pen shrugged. "Really, it's just a guess on my part," he let out a laugh. "Apologies, guess is not an intentional pun. That name of yours, Guy Guess, is an odd one at any rate!"

Guy clenched his fist. "You're forgetting one thing, Pen."

"What's that?"

The bubble began to constrict. "I still have the power to destroy you."

Pen's eyes widened. "You forgetting I can destroy you too!" he raged. The bubble on Guy's ship expanded once more.

"Yes Pen," Guy agreed. "You're forgetting another thing. I'm willing to die for something larger than myself. Are you willing to do the same?"

Pen howled like a wolf. "Blast you, Guy! I'll blast you from the sky!"

"What is it with all the poetry today?" Guy said.

"You think you're pretty funny, don't you Guy?"

"I don't know. I'll leave it to you to figure out if I'm pretty or funny."

"I'll show you something to laugh about."

Guy nodded. "I know you can do that."

Pen disappeared and reappeared on Guy's horsecraft. "I assume you did not know I could do that!"

Guy put up his fists in a defensive stance. "Yeah, you surprised me. Let's see if I can return the favor."

Guy swung a fist at Pen. It went through the giant. "Still surprising you, aren't I?" Pen said. "I can turn intangible."

Guy laughed. "You figured out some things. Let me show you what I've got in my magic novelty case!" He walked over and reached into a wall. He pulled out a backpack.

Pen's smile faded. "Is that Eerey's?"

Guy pulled the zipper. "You know it is." He reached in and pulled out Eightball, holding the large spider under its belly. Guy looked at Pen. "I think you know what this is too."

Pen turned pale and away. "Keep that bug away from me!"

Guy set Eightball on the floor. "I won't do anything with him. I'm just letting him out to play."

Pen laughed nervously. "He can't do anything to me," He said. "I'm intangible!"

Guy shrugged. "If you're so sure..."

Pen fell to his knees. "You know I'm really not! Please, put it away! I'll do anything!"

Guy sneered. "You will do anything, and I've seen what you might do. That's why I can't let you do anything more."

Eightball skittered toward Pen. Pen backed against the wall, his eyes wide as saucers. "If you let him kill me, he'll be killing Eerey too!"

"Eerey would not want to live as part of you. You've always been afraid of spiders."

Eightball rushed up to Pen's leg and attempted to bite it as Pen disappeared and reappeared on the other ship. "Ha!" he said as he looked at Guy from the viewport of Idon's horsecraft. "That creeper didn't get me!"

Guy smiled. "He didn't? Look behind you."

Pen turned to see Eerey and Idon standing there. Eerey clenched her teeth and spun in the air to deliver a kick to Pen. It connected in his midriff and he let out a huff as he staggered against the wall. He saw that he'd teleported Eightball with him. He kicked the spider off his leg. The spider rolled against the wall.

Pen smiled. "You seem angry, Eerey. Pretty tough to find out I'm a part of you isn't it?"

Eerey rushed over to Eightball and picked hugged him. "Oh Eightball! Are you okay?"

"That stupid spider," Pen said, "should be a paperweight!"

Eerey shook her head as she stood, closed fists at her side. "You think you are me Pen, but you're not. It is you who were part of a worm. You are brilliant though. I'll give you that. It seems you have figured out how to connect to others through their DNA strains.

<Author's note: I cannot tell if Eerey meant 'connect to' or 'connect two' from her notes. All necessary apologies to the reader.> You've become a Doctor Frankenstein and Doctor Who all-in-one. You still haven't created Pendragon Umbra Cryptic. Not really."

Pen frowned but did not move. Eerey continued her harangue. "You always knew a spider would be your undoing. That is why you fear them so. You spend your life trying to be anything or anyone besides yourself, Pen. It's the ultimate form self-loathing. Idon and I have accepted ourselves. We are not perfect, but we are glad for the imperfections. It makes us real. That will always escape you. You keep looking in vain for the perfect form, the greatest experience. If you can love yourself and others with all the imperfections and always try to improve, that is the greatest experience. Everything you need has always been within you, yet you continue to look elsewhere." Eerey shook her head. "The perfection you seek in others will always disappoint you. You can look like them, but you cannot be them. That's how you miss the mark."

"You're not perfect either!" Pen snarled.

"No, I am not." She turned to Idon. "Are you perfect, Idon?"

Idon shook her head.

"See Pen? Everyone is perfectly imperfect. They are all beautiful in their uniqueness. No one can be another. You are unique Pen, and a gift to yourself."

With a sneer, Pen stood to his feet and sighed. "Well," he said, "I think I'm done listening to your sermon." He dusted off his jacket while flashing his shark-teeth. "Good day." Another horsecraft, made of bronze-colored metal, appeared in the viewport on the other side from Guy's ship. "I will be taking my leave now."

Pen disappeared in a flash and reappeared in the bronze horsecraft. He waved before the ship disappeared.

Eerey turned to Idon. "Now what do we do?"

Idon walked to the viewport and looked out. "Now," she said, "we find him. Now we stop him."

"Where do find him?"

"We must find him in time, Eerey. Before we run out of time."

"We'll go back to where we know he will be," Eerey decided. "We'll go back to Gyges' fortress!"

Idon shook her head. "When you saw him at the fortress he seemed to already be travelling in time. Somehow he lost how to operate Guy's horsecraft. If we confront him at Gyges fortress he may have worked out all the possibilities."

Eerey adjusted her goggles. "He must have found the bronze horsecraft since then."

Idon nodded. "Yes. We must find out how and where he figured it out. That is the place to stop him and repair the damage."

Eerey nodded. "We should land. We don't need to be flying to travel through time."

Idon agreed. She looked toward Guy's horsecraft. "Follow us Guy. We will land. You can help search with your horsecraft. That way we can cover more time in a shorter amount of space."

Guy nodded. Idon returned to the steering wheel. The horsecraft moved toward the invisible tower. In a moment Idon landed the ship on the tower. Guy followed suit and landed next to Idon's horsecraft.

An explosion shook the invisible tower as they landed. Eerey looked down through the several invisible floors of the tower. "Lava's pouring into the tower, Idon!"

Idon put her hand on her forehead. "This is very bad. Pen will destroy this planet and perhaps time itself! We must hurry!"

CHAPTER XXII

CRYSTAL CITY

"Where and when are we going?" Eerey asked.

Idon went to the wheel of the horsecraft. It lifted into the air. "We are going to Monstrator. This time, we will forego the sightseeing tour. We must find out where that bronze horsecraft originated."

"Don't you know that already?" Eerey asked. "I thought you were a Monstrian!"

Idon looked at Eerey. "I am you, Eerey. Your potential is my reality. It is as clear as I can make it. I recall little of my life Monstrator, though I have since visited its past. I awoke in the tower with a mission in mind. The mission was to observe Earth and the potential to re-Monstrate it for colonization."

Eerey nodded. "So, are we going to LAND on Monstrator?"

Idon nodded. The horsecraft plunged through space at a fantastic speed. Venus flew by the viewport. In literally no time they approached

Monstrator and entered the atmosphere.

The light from the sun lit up the interior corners of the horsecraft. The ship stopped momentarily. Eerey felt the warmth of the sun on her face. She stared straight at the sun, smiling broadly. "It is beautiful!"

Idon nodded. "Indeed it is. We must hurry."

"I thought we had nothing but time in a time machine?"

"That is less than true," Idon maintained. "Inside this ship, we are outside of time, yet we still live by its rules. If the past is destroyed the future will disappear. You and I, both of us, will disappear with it. If time ceases existing, we will cease with it."

Idon turned to Eerey with a solemn gaze. "Since we exist, we can keep it safe. It will be extremely dangerous, and we might have to give up our lives for others. I cannot do it without you. I therefore ask you Eerey, Eridona, Idon; will you help me?"

Eerey nodded. "No question."

Idon returned to the wheel. The horsecraft flew through the multi-colored atmosphere of Monstrator. All the colors whirled in a Northern Lights fashion.

A city appeared with clear crystal buildings shimmering in the light. Their construction seemed familiar and alien at the same time. The corners of the buildings stood at 90 degrees. The light inside the crystals created all types of shapes despite, or because of, its seemingly ordinary construction. Eerey gasped at the view.

Idon nodded. "It took my breath away the first time I saw it. It is captivating. Appreciate it, Eerey, but quickly. "

"It's perfect."

"It is great, that is true." Idon replied. "It is still a planet and governed by laws of gravity and entropy. It will die out as all planets will. Perfection eludes us as long as there are lessons we have not learned. This is Monstrator's past. Its present is a much sorrier state."

Idon directed the horsecraft toward a tall building. Eerey wanted to close her eyes as the horsecraft flew right for the wall and through the crystal structure. The ship landed in a room. One wall had a kind of enormous, clockwork computer made of crystal. In total, it stood five-stories high in Eerey's estimation. The apparatus gleamed with the motion of the wheels, cogs along with other pieces that caused the machine to run.

Eerey stared at the machine in amazement. "What is this?"

"It is a computation device," Idon said. "It contains a record of all of Monstrator's known history."

"Can we download it to another computer?" Eerey asked. "I have my laptop back on Earth."

Idon shook her head. "Time is of the essence. We only need one piece of that history. We need to discover when the bronze horsecraft left Monstrator." The giantess walked to the computer and placed her hands on it.

"How long will this take?" Eerey asked.

Idon turned to her, eyes wide with surprise. "It is done! It is far less than believable!"

"What's it say?"

Idon turned to look toward the sun. "It says the ship is leaving today!"

Eerey followed Idon's gaze. Across the crystal city, a bronze horsecraft flew away from Monstrator.

Idon let out a gasp. "Quickly! To our ship! That horsecraft must be captured!"

"It looks as if another horsecraft has that exact idea!" Eerey exclaimed, pointing at a golden horsecraft flying after the bronze ship. A black horsecraft rose to follow as well. "That's Guy's horsecraft!" Eerey added. "What is going on?"

Idon rushed to their horsecraft. "We must find out!"

Idon got behind the wheel as Eerey came up the steps. They took off in pursuit of the other horsecraft. "Did the computer tell you who was on them?" Eerey asked.

Idon nodded. "It is strange a surprise. The ships are manned by Guy and Pen."

"Who's manning the gold ship?" Eerey asked.

"That is Mister Cryptic."

"I don't know why or how, but that makes sense to me."

"It makes sense to you and me both. Everything is coming together."

"Well," Eerey said, "can you track them? I've got some questions."

"It may be that Pen at least will be reluctant to answer your questions. You were pretty rough on him."

"Maybe," Eerey said. "Not half as rough as I'd like to be."

Idon stood up from the wheel. She held her hands toward the chair. "This battle is yours as much as mine. You should take the wheel."

Eerey's eyes widened as she slipped behind the wheel. The chair back went high above her head. "Will I be able to fly it?"

Idon shrugged. "Probably. It came fairly naturally the first time I tried."

Eerey smiled and grasped the wheel. The ship surged forward at her thought. "This is amazing! How do I follow the other horsecrafts?"

"The horsecraft will obey your thoughts," Idon said.

Eerey thought to the horsecraft to follow the others. "Horsecraft, follow the other horsecraft."

Idon laughed. "You need not say it aloud!"

Eerey shrugged. "I'm just getting the hang of this."

They flew toward the Earth, again passing Venus. The orb of Earth came into view. Soon, the horsecraft descended past the cloud cover. The oceans and continents became visible. The horsecraft flew down to the ocean and skimmed its surface at amazing speed.

Eerey laughed. "This is fun!"

Idon nodded. "Enjoy yourself for now. It may be that soon we are faced with incredible dangers."

"I suppose we have to save the world."

Idon shrugged. "We'll save the world just this once if that is okay with you."

"Of course it is!" Eerey laughed. "They make my favorite ice cream here!"

"Levity is good," Idon said. "It makes the gravity of the situation weigh less heavily. We now need to go to the place and time where I first picked you up."

Eerey thought about Idon's suggestion. Eerey raised the ship high above the Earth. She sent it to the time period where Idon first her picked up. The world beneath them changed. The oceans shrank to muddy pools and the rivers to dry valleys. Volcanoes roared, spewing molten lava into the air along with black smoke. Lava filled the enormous cracks that appeared in the crust of the Earth. Animals, plants, and people were nowhere to be seen. "This looks like a disaster!" Eerey remarked.

"I always was one for understatement," Idon replied. "This is the worst I've seen. The Earth is cracking like an egg. Pen has really done it this time."

"I like him even less than before," Eerey said.

"Perhaps the time for levity has passed," Idon suggested.

Eerey gritted her teeth. "It has for Pen." She scanned the skyline to see the other three horsecraft in the distance. She thought about reaching the ships. In a few moments the horsecraft entered the gathering of horsecrafts. She saw a beam from Pen's horsecraft strike Guy's black horsecraft and send it spinning downward.

"Hey!" She shouted. "Pen attacked Guy!" She turned the ship.

"Do not do so, Eerey," Idon said. "This is bigger than Guy's life. If we do not save the world, he will die with us and everything else."

Eerey gritted her teeth. "If we don't watch out for each other, I'm not sure we deserve to live." She tried to decide quickly. Pen made the decision for her. A beam from the bronze horsecraft struck Eerey's ship. The copper horsecraft rocked like a hobbyhorse. Eerey concentrated on bringing the ship back under control.

Eerey righted the horsecraft through much effort. Sweat poured of her brow. She saw Pen make another pass to attack her. The beam shot out of the bronze horsecraft. Guy's black horsecraft deflected Pen's beam with one of his own.

"Guy!" Eerey smiled. Her nose scrunched as she turned the ship to face Pen once more. "It's my move."

She fired a beam at Pen's horsecraft, sending a laser of red light through the ship. She concentrated on expanding the sphere inside Pen's horsecraft.

Pen pressed his horsecraft full-power toward Eerey's, causing huge sparks as it headed down the beam from her horsecraft.

"He'll crash into us!" Eerey said. "What will happen if he does?"

Idon shrugged. "We hope he has liability insurance."

The ship kept coming. "If there was a time when levity was inappropriate, Idon, this is it. That horsecraft is on my light beam." Eerey concentrated. The beam widened as she built up energy. A sphere of light followed the beam down and struck Pen's horsecraft.

The explosion when the sphere struck rocked Idon's horsecraft. Idon nodded with satisfaction as Pen's horsecraft fell toward the chaotic surface far below. "It looks like we got it!" Eerey said.

"I doubt it," Idon replied.

Pen's horsecraft righted itself and flew upward. Eerey stamped in frustration. "What will it take to stop him?"

"You made a sphere and a line," Idon said. "Perhaps a different shape would be effective."

Eerey nodded. "These are just stasis fields, aren't they?"

"Yes. They create a space where time does not affect movement."

"Okay," Eerey said. "I've been approaching it wrong." She concentrated hard, sweat coating her brow. A beam in the shape of a hollow tube left the horsecraft toward Pen's ship. "Let's see how the horsecraft fares when only part in a stasis field and the rest is not."

The tube struck the center of Pen's horsecraft. A horrendous sound filled the air as the ship lit up the sky with an orange light before it stopped moving.

Eerey retracted the light beam. "I think that did it for sure!"

Idon nodded as she watched the lifeless ship fall from the sky. "I think it did. That horsecraft is devoid of energy."

"That's good," Eerey said. "We have to make sure it can't be used again. How can we do that?"

Idon replied, "When in a powerless state it cannot withstand intense heat and pressure."

Eerey nodded. She captured the falling horsecraft in a bubble of red light.

"You have a plan," Idon said.

"Yes, I have a plan," Eerey replied. "You could just ask me. Your habit of never asking questions is getting annoying."

"It is," Idon agreed.

Eerey sighed. She concentrated on bringing Pen's horsecraft next to hers. Once she brought the ships side-by-side, she sent her horsecraft and Pen's plummeting into the exposed, molten surface of the Earth.

"What are you doing?"

"I'm glad you asked instead of telling me," Eerey said. "You said we may have to die to save the Earth. Well, I'm willing. I'm going to subject this ship and the other to intense heat and pressure. We're going where it's nearly as hot as the sun's surface. We're going to the center of the Earth!"

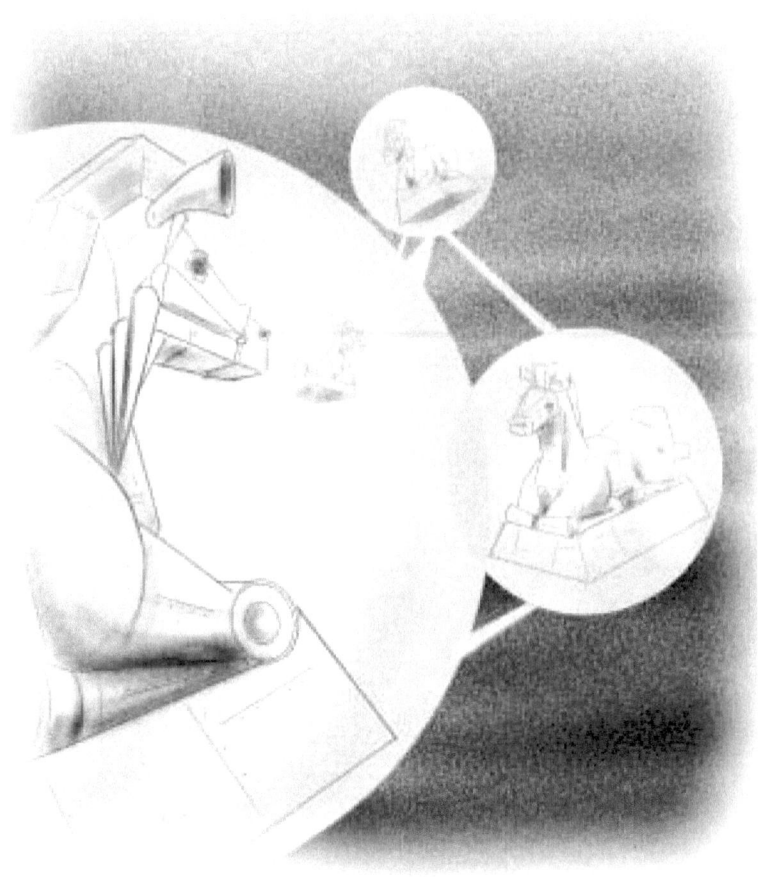

CHAPTER XXIII

WORLD ON FIRE

Riding parallel to each other, the horsecrafts struck the reddish-orange lava beneath the thick, acrid smoke. The burning orange light put off by the hot lava hurt Eerey's eyes. She squinted behind her dark goggles and pressed onward. She wiped sweat from her brow. "Can't this ship handle this heat?"

"This is unwise to attempt," Idon admitted. "My recollection of this journey is hazy."

"Do you recall any of this?" Eerey asked.

Idon shook her head.

Pen appeared suddenly, teleporting from his horsecraft. "Eridona," he hissed, "this is beyond the pale."

Idon stepped forward. "I recall purposely forgetting to send you an invite Pen."

Pen growled as he shoved Idon away. She struck the wall with force. She passed out from the blow. "This is not for you, old Erie. I have a bone to pick with this petulant child."

Eerey smiled gravely. "It's time we had this talk, Pen. It is long overdue."

"You've destroyed my horsecraft!" Pen fumed.

Eerey shook her head. "It's still there. Some brass polish will fix it right up."

Pen looked hopefully at what little he could see through the molten lava. He shook his head. "That's not funny! The metal's been drained of its abilities! Despite that, you haven't defeated me yet, Eerey!"

"What kind of creature will you become, Pen?" Eerey taunted. "Can you teleport back to the surface? It's pretty much gone."

Pen walked toward Eerey, his hands extended. "I can strangle you and take this horsecraft. It's not my favorite color, but I can live with it."

Pen tried to put his hands around Eerey's throat, but they slipped right through. Pen's eyes widened. "I can't hurt you!"

Eerey smiled. "I know. I've learned a trick or two."

"How?"

"Just by paying attention. You should try it."

Pen swung at Eerey. His fist connected on her chin. "You didn't know I could become intangible, did you?" He laughed. "I'm stronger than you!"

Eerey wiped some blood trickling from her mouth. "Wow. You're stronger than a little girl. You can become anything you want, and you're just a schoolyard bully?"

Pen tried to hit Eerey again, but this time she was ready. She ducked his blow and moved away as he stumbled forward. "You may be stronger Pen, but I'm smarter. It's not an ego thing, either." Eerey feigned boredom with a yawn. "I kinda wish you were smarter so you wouldn't bore me so much."

Pen ran after Eerey, his fist swinging against the air. "I will not be mocked!" he roared.

"My, my. All that power, and you can't even catch a little girl? You should go back to villain school."

"I will kill you!" Pen shouted. "Then, I will destroy your precious Earth!"

"Well, I think you've managed to destroy the world," Eerey stopped to catch her breath. She wiped the sweat from her brow. "Congratulations. Now see if you can kill a little girl with glasses."

Pen roared and chased after Eerey as sweat poured off his brow. "You're too smart for your own good!" he said. Eerey tried to run away, but could barely remain standing. She turned to face Pen. "Go ahead," she said between heavy breaths. "I am ready."

Pen brought his arms forward to grasp Eerey. Eightball leapt at Pen and sunk his teeth into his left arm. A blinding white flash filled the horsecraft. As the light dissipated, A Monstrian giant appeared dress in a glowing white outfit. "NO!" Pen shouted. He fell to his knees and began weeping. He stared up at the giant. Pen exclaimed. "Cab Calloway!?"

The giant smiled a broad, friendly smile. His large, white hat with tilted brim caught the light. His over-sized coat went to his ankles, matching his large, white bowtie. "It can't be!"

The giant laughed. "No way, Jay! I'm Pendragon Umbra Cryptic! I'm you!"

Pen scrunched his forehead. "You look exactly like Cab Calloway."

The giant shrugged. "I can look like anyone, son. You don't remember assimilating me this morn?" The giant shook his head. "See, you didn't recognize yourself."

"That's because you looked like Buddy Holly!" Pen said.

The Monstrian nodded. "Yeah, but it's me," the giant replied. "Or actually you. I'm a music fan, Stan. I'm the side of Pendragon you thought you killed back on Monstrator. You know, when you assimilated me and stole the bronze horsecraft. You came back the day I was going to leave Monstrator for my mission."

Pen grasped at the giant's shoes. "I didn't know!"

The giant nodded. "You didn't know you were killing yourself over nothing. Nothing is a good reason to continue punishing yourself. I know what you were looking for." The giant shrugged. "You had it all along. You just forgot. Come on now, stand up. I'm not a god. I'm just you. Good and bad. It's never too late to take the harder path and do the right thing."

Pen looked up at the giant and stood to his feet. "I hated you because I was afraid."

"Yes. There is no reason to be." The giant pressed his white-gloved fingers against Pen's chest. "It's all in here. You had everything you needed from the beginning. You just forgot."

Pen smiled and nodded. "I know now!" He closed his eyes. "Thank you." Pen snored as the giant dissipated.

Okay," Eerey said as she sat on the floor. She wiped sweat from her brow. She breathed in short gasps. "Okay. Now to get the horsecraft to the surface and let some air in and heat out."

Eerey concentrated on directing the ship. The heat made it difficult to concentrate and the horseship foundered. It moved through the lava sluggishly. She took another breath.

Idon stirred from the spot where she fell. "Can you do this Eerey?"

Eerey nodded. "I can. I just need to keep concentrating."

"That's good," Idon said. "I cannot help you."

The horsecraft pushed through the hot lava. As the ship approached the surface, the lava cooled. It became thicker and required more concentration, though there it became lighter at the same time as it moved away from the center of Earth's gravity. The intense heat inside the ship did not diminish as quickly. Eerey blinked her eyes to stay awake.

The horsecraft finally burst through the lava's surface, spraying the boiling molten rock flying through the air. With great effort, Eerey concentrated on sending the horsecraft to an earlier time period.

Exhausted from the ordeal, Eerey passed out during the transition. When she awoke she observed a rolling hill carpeted with green grass to land the horsecraft. She awoke Idon. "Idon, we've landed. Let's get out and let the horsecraft cool down."

Idon nodded and soon they were departing from the overheated ship. Eerey saw Pen's horsecraft remained attached to the side of hers, held there by the red bubble of light. It had turned to a transparent, cloudy glass. Exhausted, she lay down on the soft, cool grass and rested.

As Eerey awoke, she noticed the sun fell farther to the West and twilight. Idon stood on the hilltop as she looked down at the prostate form of Pen.

Eerey stood up and walked to Idon's side. "Is he dead?"

Idon shook her head. "Dying."

Eerey knelt by Pen and took his hand in hers. "I am sorry it had to happen this way, Pen. You had to be stopped."

Pen coughed, then smiled at Eerey knowingly. "I had to be stopped," he rasped. "I'm a great villain after all!" He coughed again. "You said I wasn't!"

Eerey nodded. "If that's what you want to be, you are a great villain. You almost destroyed the Earth after all."

"It's nice to have an accomplishment for my eulogy," Pen wheezed. "Can you say something about me?"

Eerey nodded. "I had fun when we first met, and you helped save our bacon a couple of times."

Pen waved away the notion. "I don't want people thinking I was a nice guy! That's not the whole truth. Tell them all the rotten things I've done."

Eerey shook her head. "I'll say the truth. You strived to achieve recognition without effort. You only aided others when it was to your advantage. You are without a doubt the most despicable creature I have ever had misfortune to meet. You found out at the end that you were someone great."

Pen closed his eyes and smiled. "Thank you. To understand perfectly at the end is a great feeling." He coughed. "It's too bad it didn't happen sooner. I hope you can fix it." He breathed out.

"With hope, perhaps we can fix it," Eerey whispered as she felt his hand go limp. She let it go and stood to her feet. "It wasn't a compliment," she whispered. She turned to Idon. "He's gone."

Idon nodded. "It is time to read his letter."

"Yes," Eerey agreed.

CHAPTER XXIV

VILLANOUS CONFESSION

She reached into her backpack and removed the envelope. Eightball stirred and turned around before she zipped the backpack closed. Eerey took the plain envelope, brittle and aged as it was, and opened it. The paper turned to dust and floated in the air as Eerey read the letter aloud,

"Eerey. I will not say 'I am your father' or anything of the kind. Firstly, those types of revelations are a bit overdone. For that reason and others I am pleased to say that I am not your father. Secondly, I am not your father in the familiar sense. You see, you are me and I am you, at least in part. Certainly, we are siblings of a sort. This may be something of a cliché on my part, yet it is the truth."

Eerey paused. "He was wrong there."

Idon nodded. "When someone lies to everyone, it is difficult to tell the truth from the falsehood. Pen believed what he said. It is still less than true."

Eerey continued reading. "It happened that I found it once necessary to turn to a night crawler and split myself, as I did later when I turned into a starfish. Not being able to survive long in seawater, a fish ate me. I then became a fish and went about eating other worms. Some may call my diet of worms ironic. I just laugh at the idea!

"Though I cannot recall why I turned into a worm, I am certain it was for a good reason. What I have come to realize only recently is that there is a reason for all of this. I mean for everything a reason of everything; a R.O.E. I do not know what that reason is. I know there is a reason.

"I know in the past I have done things you will think wrong or bad. I make no apologies. I have chosen my path and wish to be a true villain. If you feel bad for me, feel bad that I have not accomplished what I set out to do and am not the world's worst, or best, villain depending on how you look at it.

"I will leave that as it is. You want to know how I left a letter in the ship. You see, I have planned carefully, and you have reacted perfectly. We being a part of each other, I can anticipate your reactions as you have seen through my disguises."

"He was wrong again," Eerey said. "I simply got on the horsecraft and left with Guy. He didn't expect that."

She continued; "All of which brings us to matter of the horsecraft. It was some great time since I stepped off the airplane onto the invisible tower with you and your entourage. I was flabbergasted by the concept of time travel. I slipped away by becoming a moth after one landed on my shoulder. As you well know, I have an issue with flying. I simply cannot figure it out. I tried but was caught by the wind. Quite a harrowing time I assure you. Not long after I came across a camel and eventually a soldier. The string goes on and it all eventually led to contact with Gyges and the black horsecraft.

"I was there as an orangutaur when the horsecraft landed. The horsecraft opened, and King Gyges demanded he be allowed to go in alone. A moment later, a Monstrian giant came out followed by Gyges who yelled 'Kill him!' to his soldiers. The soldiers fell upon the Monstratrian and killed him. I quickly went to the giant's body and took a bit of his DNA before he died. I cannot change into anything from an animal that's already dead when I retrieve the DNA.

"I helped them pull the craft into this room. I returned later as a scorpion, turning into the Monstrator once inside. Once in that form, I learned all of the history of Monstrator and the Monstrators and how to operate the horsecraft.

"The orbit of Monstrator moved toward the sun faster than the other planets. Their scientists knew that life would cease to exist as it drew closer to the sun.

"As to this particular horsecraft, you saw the words on the wall when you went into it. It is, as the words S.S. AUNT ALICE suggests, built from the remains of the submarine you so recently had your adventure. When Guy turned the submarine invisible, the energy he created energized the metal. When it sunk the gorillas continued to pilot it. Because of the left-over energy it slowly turned intangible. The Gorillas continued being the seafarers they are and being intangible they never grew old and never ran out of intangible bananas. They eventually passed away. The submarine stopped being effected by Earth's gravity and drifted in space. It started sliding backward through time.

"Finally, the submarine travelled back so far that the ship slid through time to when Monstrator was near the orbit Earth is now. The Monstrator scientists caught it in a beam and drew it to their planet.

"They studied the intangible ship. Discovering its unusual properties, they used the energy from the sun so the Monstrians turn intangible. They also stabilized Monstrator's orbit.

"Invisibility was a simple by-product of the intangibility and was placed in a ring form. When the Monstrians travelled away from the sun, they could no longer remain intangible.

"Not that the Monstrator scientists concerned themselves with the problem. They made four horsecrafts from the unique metal of the Aunt Alice. They travelled to Earth and built the invisible tower. They wished to move to Earth and become tangible, yet the planet proved too wild for them. They abandoned their efforts. Apparently, they sent Idon to discover if efforts to re-Monstrate Earth might be feasible."

"All this I gathered while riding through time in the black horsecraft. My DNA waned. I was forced to land the horsecraft as I could no longer control it without Monstrian DNA. It landed outside the fortress of King Gyges, where and when it had landed before. I discovered I had taken the form of the giant! Figuring out what was happening, I opened the stairs and waited. King Gyges entered and after some conversation, we shook hands. That gave me the DNA I needed. I then took his form and put an illusion on him to look like the Monstrian. He rushed out shouting 'Kill him! Kill him!' The orangutaurs thought I shouted it as my lips moved and I looked like Gyges. The Monstrian they killed was Gyges! He even ordered his own execution!

"After that, I ordered the orangutaurs, even myself disguised as an orangutaur, to drag the horsecraft to the fortress. I did not tell my orangutaur self as that would confuse matters. This letter might be confusing enough already.

"That details some of my adventures, and possibly clears things up for you. Figuring out the time was close to when you would arrive at the invisible tower, I put this letter in the horsecraft. I knew you would come for Guy as the Aunt Alice drew him through affinity to the horsecraft version of it. I thought to have you help me repair the horsecraft, for if you do not, I will kill you and Guy both. So, get to work. Sincerely, PEN"

"He thought that would get me to help him? He doesn't know me very well, does he?"

"Apparently less than he thought he did. His ego proved to be his downfall."

Eerey crumpled the letter. "I can't tell how much of this letter is to be believed. He was an insane liar, and believed his own lies. It reads like a fever dream."

Idon sighed and looked at the sun. "It matters little now. He is dead and the future is set right."

Eerey scratched her head. "Why was he in the bronze horsecraft? He did not mention that in his letter."

Idon pointed at the sky. Mr. Cryptic's gold horsecraft approached. "Perhaps Mister Cryptic can enlighten us."

CHAPTER XXV
EULOGY FOR AN UNKNOWN

The horsecraft gleamed in the twilight as it landed without perceptible noise. The staircase descended and Mr. Cryptic walked down the steps in full health. He wore a dark maroon, pinstripe suit over his seven-foot-tall frame. His long gray hair flowed over his shoulders. Behind him, Loofah-the-orangutan on the back of Loofah-the-horse came down the stairs.

Eerey smiled. "Hi Mister Cryptic!" She waved at Loofah. "Hi Loofah and horse."

"My name's Silver," Silver grumbled.

Eerey looked at Mr. Cryptic. "You're doing okay after being bandaged up."

Mr. Cryptic delivered a fond smile. "Hello Eerey. I see I am too late." He looked down at the Elvis-impersonator, Monstrian body of Pen. His face fell. "So sorry, my brother Pendragon."

"Your brother?" Eerey asked.

Mr. Cryptic looked at the sky and closed his eyes. "When a Monstrian comes to Earth, they do not only become tangible. They also forget their past life."

Eerey adjusted her goggles. "Like a doppelganger?"

Mr. Cryptic met Eerey's gaze. "Yes. A doppelganger sometimes forgets when they take a simple form like that of an earthworm. A doppelganger usually takes a human form. Pendragon used a device to accomplish the changes into many different kinds of animals. He designed it to adapt to Earth's conditions and experiment with suitable bodies for the Monstrians. Unfortunately, he forgot why he came. His being physical, combined with the ability to change, made him hungry for power."

"Why didn't you tell him?" Eerey asked.

"I discovered Pen's designs to destroy the world and used the horsecraft I discovered hidden in the Cryptoid Zoo. I used it to help you fight in the battle you just finished. I was wounded in that battle. The horsecraft returned me to the last place it left, the Cryptoid Zoo. After I bandaged my severe wounds, I managed to steer the horsecraft into the cargo hold of your parent's plane. I fell into a deep hibernation to recuperate. They went in search for you and found you on the Kraken. The rest you know already."

"Okay," Eerey said, "that explains some of it. What about Guy?"

"Guy was an infant who swallowed the ring of King Gyges," Mr. Cryptic replied. "It turned him invisible, which saved his life. He was afraid, so he stayed hidden. He scrounged enough food to get by. Someone brought him to the 1990s. His education came from silent observation as he went to school, unbeknownst to the faculty. I brought him to the zoo to keep him safe, but lost him before I could explain. He didn't trust people." Mr. Cryptic looked at the body of Pen. "I think it was sometimes the wisest thing he could do."

"Why did Guy get the black horsecraft?" Eerey asked.

Mr. Cryptic let out his breath. "The metal was tuned to Guy. When Guy turned the Aunt Alice intangible, he became attached to it."

"I saw him leave Monstrator in it!" Eerey said.

"Yes. I was the Monstrator scientist that created the horsecraft."

"Why are they shaped like horses?" Silver asked.

"Because," Mr. Cryptic smiled, "I became friends with a talking horse who helped me build it." He patted Silver's head.

"You can't take Silver!" Loofah protested, wrapping his orangutan arms around the horse's neck. "We're attached."

Silver shook his head. "Not anymore, monkey-breath."

Mr. Cryptic laughed. "You're both going with me to Monstrator. That is, if you want."

Loofah nodded. "If Silver's going, so am I."

"Yeah," Silver replied in a surly manner. "I don't want to lose the dumb mug. Can you tell us how we became an orangutaur in the first place?"

"That's simple," Mr. Cryptic said. "Pen designed you and many other creatures when looking for suitable forms for the Monstrians to become. He even made minotaurs and large spiders. The spiders were meant to be a fail-safe to keep these creations from becoming too dangerous. The spiders's bite could break the artificial DNA strands."

Eerey nodded. "That's why Pen hated them! They could break his doppelganger abilities. Were all the creatures made by Pen?"

Mr. Cryptic shook his head. "No. There are still mysteries, even to the Monstrians. I was sent to collect suitable lifeforms of the planet while Pendragon worked on the creation aspect. Pendragon never could make anything new. He could combine, but he still needed DNA for the building blocks."

"Anything else?" Eerey asked.

"Of course there is more. There are more interesting yet trivial details." Mr. Cryptic looked at Pen's body. "We have a funeral to attend."

"Where should we bury him?" Loofah asked.

"We must bury him in his horsecraft." Mr. Cryptic replied.

Guy arrived as they were carrying Pen's body into the horsecraft. He landed next to the copper horsecraft and came over to help. "Can I help?" he asked.

Eerey carried the giant's left leg as Mister Cryptic and Idon carried Pen's upper body. "Yes," Eerey replied. "Carry his right leg."

Guy grasped the other leg. They carried the body up the stairs and laid it on the giant chair, already arranged into a reclining position.

After arrange Pen's collar and hair, Eerey followed the others as they left the horsecraft. The horse's head closed to cover the stairs again. Mr. Cryptic walked to the side of the horsecraft.

He gave the horsecraft a light tap with his black-gloved fingertip as Idon sang a high note pleasing to the ears. A straight crack appeared in the center of the horsecraft. It continued around the craft, separating the top from the bottom like a coffin lid.

"How did you do that?" Loofah asked.

Mr. Cryptic shrugged. "Will you give the eulogy, Eerey?"

"Me?" she asked. "I hardly knew him. I hardly liked him."

Mr. Cryptic nodded. "I thought those would be his wishes."

Eerey sighed and removed her goggles. She folded her hands and stood next to the horsecraft. "Pendragon Umbra Cryptic," she started, "told me before he died that he wanted me to say he was a bad person and that he was evil. I have just said it. I want to point out that the Pendragon I knew was a vile and despicable person not to be trusted.

"I also want to point out that, until recently, I never knew there was another side of Pendragon, and that side is one on which I cannot comment much. That was the side that was the brother of Mister Cryptic, and I assume he was kind and interested in the welfare of others. There were moments with Pen I enjoyed before I knew how villainous he'd become.

"When he forgot who he was, he became lost, sick, dishonest, and driven mad with ambition. In the illness, he despised and lied to himself and others incessantly. In life, I didn't like him and he tried to kill me on several occasions. In death, I hope that he is at peace."

The others walked to the horsecraft one-by-one and observed Pen's body inside. They walked down the hill. Eerey stood next to the horsecraft.

Mr. Cryptic walked over and stood next to her. "Are you doing well, Eerey?"

Eerey shook her head, a small tear falling down her cheek. "I know there is no reason to mourn Pen from my experiences with him. He is the first person I know that died. When I thought Guy was dead it hurt a lot. Why Pen though?"

Mr. Cryptic placed his hand on her shoulder. "Your heart is big enough to care about someone you hated, I guess."

Eerey nodded. "I guess that's it. Or maybe it's the pressure I've gone through." She put her hand on the glass. "I don't know. Can I be alone for a moment?"

Mr. Cryptic nodded. He walked down the hill to join the others. Eerey dropped her head. "Goodbye, Pen. I can't explain, but I'm sorry you're gone." She took her hand off the glass and slowly walked away. The makeshift sarcophagus stood alone on the grassy hillside.

Idon met her along the way. "Let us return to the horsecraft."

Eerey nodded. The pair of them boarded the copper horsecraft in silence. When the ship was in the air, Idon turned it and fired at Pen's sarcophagus. The ground rumbled and cracked open. It swallowed the sarcophagus before closing again.

"Why did you do that?" Eerey asked.

"That will prepare the future," Idon said. "Now, in years to come the shepherd who was Gyges' ancestor will find the sarcophagus. He will take the ring from the hand of Pen. All that has happened will happen."

The horsecraft moved through time at Idon's thought. She hovered by the invisible tower and fired a beam at it. "It's going intangible!" Eerey said.

Idon smiled. "It is nearly finished. The tower is not usable." The giantess landed the horsecraft. Eerey and Idon walked onto the ground where the now intangible tower rested. Eerey looked up at it, barely seeing its outline.

I will leave you now, Eerey."

Eerey looked at Idon. "You're translucent, Idon!"

Idon nodded. "I am fading."

"Why?" Eerey asked.

Idon smiled. "Because, the events that led you to become me are slipping away."

"I don't want you to go away!" Eerey said.

"I will be greater for it, as I am you," Idon explained. "I am certain you will be great. Perhaps greater than I am now."

"Will you die?" Eerey asked.

Idon shook her head. "I will not. I am only fading into another you, Eerey." Her voice became hollow as her image faded. "Do well, Eerey. My life depends on you." She smiled and faded into nothingness.

"Idon!" Eerey shouted. Then she thought of the smile of the giantess. She smiled that same smile. "I don't know what the future holds," she said to herself. "I don't know all the mysteries, and I don't know everything in the darkness." She looked at the countryside and smiled. "It will be an adventure to find out!" She turned to Idon's horsecraft. It faded before her eyes and disappeared.

Mr. Cryptic's horsecraft appeared and landed next inside the intangible tower. The head opened and formed the stairs. Mr. Cryptic descended with Guy, Loofah, Silver, and King Benedict.

"Hello again Eerey," Mr. Cryptic said. "We were wondering where you went."

"Idon and I went for a ride." Eerey said. She walked to King Benedict. "Are you returning with us, Edict?"

King Benedict shook his head. He hugged Eerey for a moment, then let her go. "I can't Eerey. I just had to say goodbye."

Eerey nodded and smiled. "I know. I'm so proud of you!"

"Hey!" King Benedict said. "You're not wearing your sunglasses! I thought you'd take the glasses back from Pen. Didn't you recognize them?"

Eerey smiled and glanced at the sun. "I knew they were the ones you lost. They were the reason we ended up at the Cryptoid Zoo in the first place." She shrugged. "I don't need them anymore, and I thought Pen should be buried with them. I left them in his pocket. How did he get them in the first place?"

Edict shrugged. "I guess we won't know everything just yet."

Eerey nodded. "I'm not sure I want to know everything. Light doesn't hurt as much anymore, Edict. I've seen the sun for what it is." She looked at her feet. "I'm not afraid of the dark anymore either. I don't know who I am yet, yet I know who I might be."

King Benedict nodded. "I've seen you for what you are, Eerey. A beautiful sun all your own."

A plane's engines roared on the horizon. Eerey hugged King Benedict with a tear in her eye. "That's my ride, cuz. Mom and dad will take me home." She stepped away and smiled. "You're still a troglodyte, you know."

Edict smiled and nodded. "I know. Pretty cool, isn't it?"

Eerey stared at the sun. "Yeah, cuz. It is. Everything is pretty cool."

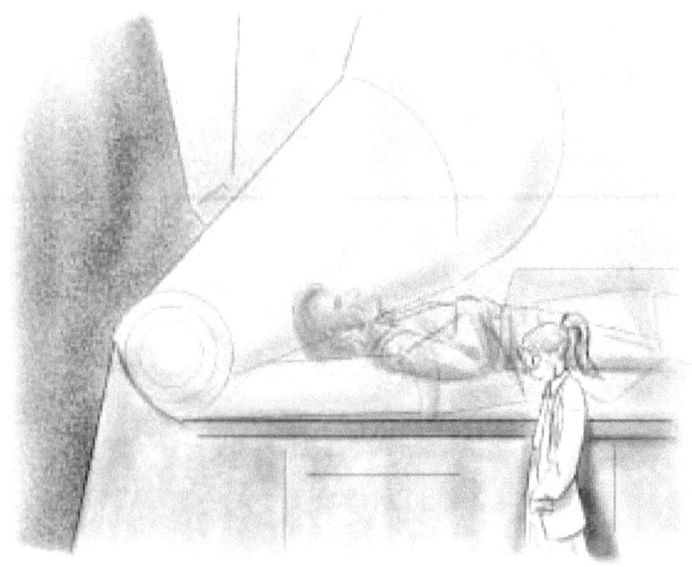

www.ingramcontent.com/pod-product-compliance
Lightning Source LLC
Chambersburg PA
CBHW030510260626
47157CB00005B/1724